"I wouldn't think a man like you would be interested in cuddling,"

Liz told Joe.

"Define 'a man like you.'"

"An upwardly mobile businessman, single and—" She hesitated.

"And?" he prompted, one dark, well-formed eyebrow lifting with the question.

She'd been about to say "attractive," but didn't dare. "And busy."

"That's all true. Although I'd like to know how you knew I was single."

The flirtatious manner was a big clue, although why she couldn't say. Another lesson from her past experience was that flirting wasn't exclusive to single men. Married ones could philander at the drop of a hat or the swish of a skirt, too.

"It was just a hunch...until now."

Dear Reader,

The year 2000 marks the twentieth anniversary of Silhouette Books! Ever since May 1980, Silhouette Books—and its flagship line, Silhouette Romance—has published the best in contemporary category romance fiction. And the year's stellar lineups across *all* Silhouette series continue that tradition.

This month in Silhouette Romance, Susan Meier unveils her miniseries BREWSTER BABY BOOM, in which three brothers confront instant fatherhood after inheriting six-month-old triplets! First up is *The Baby Bequest,* in which Evan Brewster does diaper duty…and learns a thing or two about love from his much-younger, mommy-in-the-making assistant. In Teresa Southwick's charming new Silhouette Romance novel, a tall, dark and handsome man decides to woo a jaded nurse *With a Little T.L.C. The Sheik's Solution* is a green-card marriage to his efficient secretary in this lavish fairy tale from Barbara McMahon.

Elizabeth Harbison's CINDERELLA BRIDES series continues with the magnificent *Annie and the Prince.* In Cara Colter's dramatic *A Babe in the Woods,* a mystery man arrives on a reclusive woman's doorstep with a babe on his back—and a gun in his backpack! Then we have a man without a memory who returns to his *Prim, Proper… Pregnant* former fiancée—this unique story by Alice Sharpe is a must-read for those who love twists and turns.

In coming months, look for special titles by longtime favorites Diana Palmer, Joan Hohl, Kasey Michaels, Dixie Browning, Phyllis Halldorson and Tracy Sinclair, as well as many newer but equally loved authors. It's an exciting year for Silhouette Books, and we invite you to join the celebration!

Happy reading!

Mary-Theresa Hussey

Mary-Theresa Hussey
Senior Editor

Please address questions and book requests to:
Silhouette Reader Service
U.S.: 3010 Walden Ave., P.O. Box 1325, Buffalo, NY 14269
Canadian: P.O. Box 609, Fort Erie, Ont. L2A 5X3

WITH A LITTLE T.L.C.

Teresa Southwick

Silhouette
ROMANCE™
Published by Silhouette Books
America's Publisher of Contemporary Romance

For Andrea Pascale—your encouragement, support,
friendship and love mean more than I can say. My
gratitude for sharing your little Valerie with her "outlaw"
cousin. The refresher course in baby stuff added so much
to this book. Many thanks.

 SILHOUETTE BOOKS

ISBN 0-373-19421-8

WITH A LITTLE T.L.C.

Copyright © 2000 by Teresa Ann Southwick

Visit us at www.romance.net

Printed in U.S.A.

TERESA SOUTHWICK

is a native Californian who has recently moved to Texas. Living with her husband of twenty-five years and two handsome sons, she is surrounded by heroes. Reading has been her passion since she was a girl. She couldn't be more delighted that her dream of writing full-time has come true. Her favorite things include: holding a baby, the fragrance of jasmine, walks on the beach, the patter of rain on the roof and, above all—happy endings.

Teresa also writes historical romance novels under the same name.

Dear Reader,

If there's a woman anywhere who can resist the sight of a hunky guy holding an infant, I'll eat my computer. On second thought, I'll make her a heroine with enough baggage to tour the continental United States. In fact, I did just that in *With a Little T.L.C.*

I've always loved babies. Even after raising my two sons, the baby bug isn't out of my system. For a long time now, I've wanted to be a volunteer in a newborn nursery. Few things come to mind that are as rewarding as listening to the sounds of a baby as you hold that small, warm body close. Even better is knowing that something so simple can make an important impact on a new life. Studies have been done documenting the critical role of touch in a newborn's ability to thrive. Unfortunately, I never seem to have enough time to indulge my purely selfish need to cuddle babies.

But I'm a writer. I can send my heroine where I don't have time to go. Or, better yet, my hero. The challenge was irresistible. We take it for granted that women are nurturers. But why would a man, especially a good-looking bachelor like Joe Marchetti, spend time holding babies? Remember that heroine with all the baggage? Nurse Liz Anderson can't help being cynical about her newest volunteer cuddler. Is he just a guy with a scheme to meet women? Or is he really as incredibly wonderful as he seems?

The only thing more rewarding than holding a baby is writing about someone else who holds them. It was fun discovering right along with Joe and Liz that even the most cynical heart can be healed *With a Little T.L.C.* Enjoy!

Teresa Southwick

Chapter One

"**Y**ou want to be a cuddler?"

Nurse Liz Anderson stared at the gentleman on the other side of her desk. And she did it without gawking, she thought proudly. Not easy when the man gave new meaning to the phrase tall, dark and handsome. Six feet if he was an inch. Brown almost black eyes full of intensity, charm, and humor in equal parts. And so handsome she was grateful that her voice had worked to form the words into a question.

"You sound shocked," he said.

"That's because I am."

He folded his arms over a mighty impressive chest. Almost a year ago she had dragged him out of his sister's hospital room by his ear because he balked at leaving when visiting hours were over. Considering that impressive chest, how in the world had she managed to do that?

"Why should my intentions surprise you?"

Those words spoken in that deep voice mobilized

tingles that skittered down her neck and across her shoulders.

"It's not every day that I get that kind of offer from a man."

"It's their loss."

A flirt, she thought warily. She'd run into the type before and knew enough to steer clear. "I take cuddling very seriously, Mr. Marchetti."

"You remember me," he said, rubbing his ear. "I wondered if you did."

He grinned, a pleased expression that showed off a masterful job of orthodontia or sensational genes. She wasn't sure which. But any second she expected a diamondlike sparkle from his teeth, a movie hero come to life. In any case, she thanked her lucky stars that she was already sitting. It wouldn't take much to knock her on her keister.

"You're pretty unforgettable," she muttered softly.

"Am I?" he answered, his smile growing wider.

She hadn't meant for him to hear that. Apparently all his flaws were in character because his hearing was pretty darn good.

Instead of lowering his hunky frame into one of the two chairs provided for visitors, he sat on the corner of her desk. Proving to her, as if she needed more proof after their one and only meeting, that he was a rule-breaker.

Now he sat a few scant inches from her. His tie was loose and the top button of his white dress shirt undone, allowing a couple of chest hairs to peek out. He'd rolled up his long sleeves revealing strong, tanned forearms. The gray fabric of his slacks pulled tight across his muscular thighs. His cologne added the deathblow to her composure. The wonderful masculine scent surrounded her, adding stomach flutters to her shoulder tingles.

On top of that, she could see the sexy five o'clock shadow on his cheeks and jaw. She glanced at the clock on her desk—6:30 p.m. Wasn't it past time for him to go home and shave?

Realizing she'd been staring, Liz resisted the urge to shake her head and clear it. No point in giving a man like him more fuel for his over-inflated ego. She knew he'd asked her a question. Now if only she could remember what he'd said, she would answer appropriately.

As if he could read her mind, he asked, "What else do you remember about me?"

That he'd charmed her by teasingly threatening to lock her in the broom closet when she'd told him visiting hours were over. That he had dated one of the nurses and dumped her in a nasty, hurtful way. Liz didn't especially like the woman but no one deserved to find the man they were involved with in bed with another woman.

"I remember that you left here with a beautiful blonde," she said.

He frowned for a moment as if he was trying to recall. Then he nodded. "My secretary. She'd left her husband in the car. They'd brought a gift for my sister's baby."

Liz didn't really care what kind of relationship he had with the woman. That was his business. She had a program to run. "Now let me ask you a question."

"All right."

"Are you really here to be a cuddler?"

"Yes." He pointed to the completed, orange volunteer form he'd handed her when he walked into her office. "It says so right there."

"Holding the babies?" she confirmed.

He nodded. "That's my intention."

"I just wanted to make sure we were talking about the same thing."

Because it was tough to believe *he* would be interested in spending time with infants. The last time she'd seen him in the hospital he'd hit on one of the nurses, dated then dumped her. Ninety-nine percent of her cuddlers were nurturing women who loved holding babies. The other one percent were retired men looking for something to fill their time. Then in walks Joe Marchetti, a proven playboy and flirt. What was she supposed to think when he plunked his volunteer paperwork down on her desk?

"Do you know what's involved, Mr. Marchetti?"

"Joe, Miss…"

"I beg your pardon?"

He looked at the gold, upright name plate resting on her desk. "Liz," he said, then met her gaze. "Call me Joe."

With every ounce of willpower, fortitude and any other character attributes she possessed, she resisted the power of the charming look he leveled at her. "All right, Joe," she said with more calm than she felt. "I'll ask you again. Do you know what's involved?"

"Yeah, I think so."

She leaned back in her chair, a move designed to look casual, professional, and in control. The first two weren't a problem. The last was tougher to pull off. "I wouldn't think a man like you would be interested."

"Define 'a man like you.'"

"An upwardly mobile businessman, single and—" She hesitated.

"And?" he prompted, one dark, well-formed eyebrow lifting with the question.

She'd been about to say attractive. "And busy."

"That's all true. Although I'd like to know how you knew I was single."

The flirtatious manner was a big clue, although why she couldn't say. Another lesson from her past experience was that flirting wasn't exclusive to single men. Married ones could philander at the drop of a hat or the swish of a skirt too.

But she merely answered, "You're not wearing a wedding band." Then she held up his filled-out volunteer form. "And it says so here."

He glanced at the sheet of paper and then his hand. She followed his gaze and didn't miss the fact that his fingers were long and there was a great deal of harnessed strength in his hand and wrist.

"I'm getting the impression that you doubt my sincerity. How can you judge me based on one meeting?"

"When your sister was a patient here," she clarified.

"After my niece was born," he added, rubbing his ear again.

She grinned, remembering the incident. "You were breaking the rules. Visiting hours were over."

"A simple 'please leave' would have sufficed," he said, feigning indignation. "You didn't have to yank my ear off."

She couldn't help laughing. "Aren't we being a tad melodramatic?"

"Marchettis never do anything halfway. Don't say I didn't warn you."

"Why would I need a warning?"

"Because you're the nurse in charge of the cuddlers and I'm signing up to volunteer. We'll be seeing a lot of each other."

"You think so?"

"Yes."

"Look, Joe. This program isn't fluff and feathers. Children need the best possible start in this cold, cruel world. Statistics prove that babies stimulated by touch gain weight faster."

"So I've heard."

"They cry less, have more even temperaments, sleep better and are more likely to calm and console themselves without intervention."

"I understand."

"People who aren't touched much as children don't touch much as adults and the cycle continues. The volunteers work with babies from at-risk families. This program is designed to break that cycle."

"Hey, I'm a sure thing. I'm here to do my bit. You don't have to convince me."

"No. But we have to count on you."

"What does that mean?"

"Let me ask you something first," she said.

"Okay. I'm all ears," he said, rubbing the one she'd yanked.

Liz swallowed the smile that hovered, refusing to let his clever pun distract her. "Why do you want to be a cuddler?"

He looked thoughtful, as if remembering something. "After my niece was born and you bounced me out of my sister's room, I wandered by the newborn nursery. It was just before they shut the curtains and your staff left them open a little longer for me.''

Considering his movie star good looks, Liz couldn't blame them.

"I watched the volunteers holding the babies," he continued. "And I talked to one of the nurses on duty that night who explained everything you just said. I was impressed," he finished.

When he mentioned the nurse, Liz's interest piqued. That was it. He was on the make and figured a hospital was a good place to meet women. She'd been burned like that before. What other reason could a guy like him have for being here?

"But if I remember rightly, your sister had her baby almost a year ago. As the saying goes, what took you so long?"

He shrugged. "Time got away from me."

"So why now?"

A shadow crossed his face as he remembered. "My secretary gave birth recently, a very small baby. It turned out that she was a failure-to-thrive infant."

"That's rough," Liz said, sincerely sympathetic. "What happened?"

"She's doing okay now, but they came too close to losing her. It took extra attention and stimulation. Not to mention that I lost the best secretary I've ever had."

"Really?"

"She quit because she didn't have family to leave the child with and didn't trust anyone else. I admire her commitment because they'll have it tough financially. Anyway, the point is that after the birth, and during the extra time in the hospital, she couldn't hold the baby twenty-four hours a day. The cuddlers filled in and made a difference. I decided there was no time like the present to do something worthwhile.''

"I'm glad the baby is doing well," Liz said. "But think about this. We integrate our volunteers into the schedule. The nurses count on them to pick up the slack when it gets busy. You've seen firsthand how important it is that they show up."

He frowned. "And your point is?"

"You're a single guy with a busy social calendar."

"And how would you know that?"

"Because you look like—" She stopped. What was this need she had to keep tossing him crumbs that would swell his head to the point where finding a hat to fit would be impossible?

"Never mind," she said. "Picture this scenario— you meet someone and you'd like to take her out on the spur of the moment. But you're scheduled to be here with the babies." She held one hand out. "Here we have Miss Nubile." She held out her other hand. "And here we have Miss Crankypants Infant screaming her head off. Which female do you think you'd pick?"

He scratched his chin. "Tough choice. Is Miss Nubile a blond or a brunette?"

"Which are you more partial to?"

"Tall redheads."

With an involuntary flash of disappointment, Liz figured a short brunette like herself was safe from him. "Okay, let's make Miss Nubile a tall, titian-haired temptress."

"Okay, let's."

"I knew you were impossible the first time we met."

"Thank you very much," he said brightly.

She sighed, shaking her head in exasperation. "My point is that when you don't show up because you and Miss Nubile are tripping the light fantastic somewhere, it's the babies who lose out. The role of touch is critical in child development. We need people we can count on for this program."

"You're prejudging me."

"Not you specifically, but men in general—"

"So this third degree has to do with the fact that I'm a man."

More than you could possibly imagine, she thought. But she only said, "Our average volunteer is female."

"Aren't there laws against gender discrimination?"

"Not discrimination. A screening process to protect the babies."

"I would never hurt them."

"I'm not suggesting you would deliberately harm them, but neglect—"

He stood suddenly and his agreeable, flirtatious facade disappeared. "I don't neglect children, Liz. I firmly believe that they are our most precious natural resource."

Funny, she thought. She liked his anger more than his charm. She believed it. She stood too. "That's something we see eye-to-eye on."

"By definition I thought you had to take anyone who shows up."

"True. But I won't approve any volunteer who might reflect badly on the program. It's not firmly established yet."

"No?"

She shook her head. "It's just about a year old. We're coming up for review soon. Some members of the hospital Board of Directors feel the volunteers could be better used elsewhere. I don't want to give them any ammunition to cancel the cuddlers. I have to insist on high standards."

He looked down at her, way down. "Spell it out."

"Reliability is a must. And a minimum commitment of one three hour shift a week. We require you to work four weeks in the newborn nursery before going to the Neonatal Intensive Care." She shrugged. "Those are the rules."

"You've got yourself a new recruit. When is the orientation?"

"Saturday. Ten a.m. Sharp." She glanced at his paperwork, making sure he'd filled it out completely. "Tardiness isn't an excuse."

"I'll be here."

"Read and sign the back of this please," she said, sliding the paper across her desk.

He picked it up and scanned the words. Liz knew it was an agreement to adhere to all hospital rules of safety and confidentiality. It also said a volunteer could be terminated from the program for any reason deemed sufficient by the Director of Volunteers. She didn't suppose Essie Martinez would consider booting Joe Marchetti before he started because he was too good-looking.

"May I borrow your pen?" he asked.

Hoping she wasn't making a big mistake, she handed him one and he signed the form. "So we'll see you bright and early Saturday morning?" she asked.

"I'll be here."

She gathered a file from her desk and started for the door. "Now, if you'll excuse me—"

"Where are you off to in such a hurry? Hot date?" he asked, preceding her out the door.

"Sort of. I moderate a new mothers' support group on Tuesday and Thursday evenings." She thought of something as she locked her office. "Sooner or later all the cuddlers are required to attend. I think it gives the program some continuity. Maybe you would like to join us now? Unless you have somewhere to go?"

"No, now is fine," he said without hesitation.

Good, she thought, wondering if this would scare him off. It was never too early to separate the men from the boys, test his mettle. If he was going to chicken out, better sooner than later.

Joe sat in a gray plastic chair at a long table in the front of classroom 2 and watched Liz. Wearing navy slacks and a matching blazer with a bright yellow sweater underneath, she looked stylish and professional as she stood at the door greeting everyone. Women filed in, most of them carrying infants, all of them looking tired.

He studied Ms. Liz Anderson. She was a little thing, which had wounded his male pride when she'd yanked him out of Rosie's room by his ear. But it was that moxie that had gotten his attention. She was attractive, but not one of those women who gave men whiplash when she walked down the street. Her hair, an ordinary shade of brown, was cut pixie short. Which suited her. Big hazel eyes dominated her small face. If he had to choose a word to describe her it would be cute.

The next one that popped into his mind was wary.

With him a few moments before, she'd been pleasant enough, but he'd bet all of his profit shares in

Marchetti's, Inc. that she didn't want him in her cuddlers program. She expected him to welsh on his promise. His gut told him there was more to it than that. Which made him wonder why she'd asked him to sit in on the parent's support group.

He noticed that her manner with the new mothers was warm and pleasant. Everyone got a hug. And when she looked at the babies, her face grew soft, with a glowing tenderness that made her beautiful. He wondered if she had children of her own. She wasn't wearing a wedding ring—he'd made it a point to look. But that didn't necessarily mean she was attached— or unattached.

"I guess we should start," Liz said, walking to the front of the room.

Several new mothers holding their babies sat around the long table, blankets, diapers and bags placed haphazardly on chairs in between them. They watched Liz as she made her way to the lectern with the chalkboard behind it. Joe sat in the chair closest to her.

She met his gaze. "We have a guest tonight. Ladies, this is Joe Marchetti. He's interested in joining the cuddlers program here at the hospital."

He nodded to the women settling themselves. Some were discreetly nursing their infants. Some were standing, rocking from side to side. The lucky ones sat with sleeping babies in their arms. "Hi," he said. He'd never understood the expression "fish out of water" better than he did at this moment.

Liz cleared her throat. "We'll leave the door open. There are always stragglers. You all know that with a new baby there's no guarantee of getting anywhere on time."

He leaned over to her and whispered, "Would any of those stragglers happen to be fathers?"

"This is a new *mothers'* support group." Liz shrugged.

"Ah," he answered. "I guess I just assumed some dads would come along."

"Sometimes they do," she said. "And they're always welcome. But in most cases, women are the primary caretakers, and the one whose life is most impacted with the responsibility of caring for and feeding the infant. Which reminds me. Andie, how are you doing with nursing Valerie this week? Is it going any better?"

"I think so." A dark-haired woman on the other side of the table spoke up. She had circles under her eyes, and a denim shirt that looked as if it had spent several weeks at the bottom of the ironing basket. "I called some of the people you suggested, Liz. I think Val has a shallow latch and as long as I make sure she's secure, I'm not as sore."

Joe concentrated on sitting still and looking impassive. All of this was the most natural thing in the world. His sister had nursed in front of him without embarrassment. There was no reason to be uncomfortable.

"Good." Liz nodded at the woman with satisfaction. "Anyone have any questions, problems they'd like to bring up for discussion?"

A blonde raised her hand. She was discreetly nursing her baby with a light blanket thrown over her shoulder. "What is it, Barbara?" Liz asked.

"My husband is concerned about bringing Tommy into bed with us," Barbara started, with a quick loving glance at the child in her arms. "I explained that when he wakes up in the middle of the night, it's easier if I can doze while he nurses. I get more sleep that way. But he, my husband," she clarified, "is afraid that it'll start a habit and the baby will go off to college before we get any privacy. If you know what I mean," she finished.

Joe felt everyone in the room look at him, including Liz. They were waiting for a reaction. So, this was a test. He decided he could act one of two ways. Embarrassed at such intimate discussion, or treat it as the earthy part of life it was. The woman who'd initiated the question had done it of her own free will. She wasn't put off by his presence. Why should he be uncomfortable?

"A child's needs versus intimacy is a dilemma that a lot of couples face," Liz said. "Since we have a guest of the male persuasion, and access to his point of view, what do you think about asking him? Mr. Marchetti, would you care to comment?"

He stood and cleared his throat. "I've never been married, but my parents have been together for going on thirty-six years. According to my mother, it's important for a man and woman to work on their relationship. That's the foundation of the family. If it's weak, the first crisis will topple everything."

"Good advice," Liz said, a subtle note of surprise in her voice. "But when you add a demanding new baby to the dynamic, whose needs take precedence? How do you deal with that? What about taking the child into bed?"

Joe watched the majority of women nod questioningly. Now he knew that Liz was putting him on the spot, deliberately testing him. He couldn't blame her. This was her "baby," her territory, her sphere of expertise. And he *was* a fish out of water. However, he'd always been a good test-taker. And he didn't turn his back on a challenge. He had something to prove to Nurse Ratchett. Thinking back, he tried to remember what Rosie had said when her daughter was an infant.

He cleared his throat. "At bedtime start the baby out in his or her own bed. If they wake up during the night and it doesn't look good for getting them to sleep easily, then you have to make a decision about whether or not to take them in with you."

A general murmur went up as the women commented to each other. Since they were nodding their heads and smiling, Joe figured he'd done good.

Another woman raised her hand. "Mr. Marchetti, I like bringing the baby in bed with us. I want to know that he's all right and to strengthen the family bonds. My husband doesn't mind. But lately he's been wondering when, you know, he and I can…well, you know," she finished with a shrug and shy smile.

Keep it light, he told himself. Don't let on that you'd rather be shooting hoops or pumping iron. Anything *but* advising new mothers about "you know." "I guess you're referring to what my mother calls 'the wild thing.'" They all laughed, easing the mood. "When the baby goes to sleep and the two of you are alone opportunity knocks. Answer the door," he said simply.

"What if you have other children?" someone asked.

"If you're lucky enough to have grandparents to take over, ask them for help and go to the cabin in the mountains like my folks did. If you don't have that support, try to find a routine that puts the kids in bed early so that you and your husband have time for each other.''

Just then, Barbara's baby, who had finished eating, began to wail. She stood and rocked him from side to side. "It's not easy to find a routine. Every time we do, the master," she said glancing at the unhappy infant, "changes the rules."

"Mind if I try?" he asked. After fielding the questions he just had, he figured he'd take his chances with the little guy.

"Are you kidding?" Barbara answered. "Be my guest." She held out the child.

Joe walked over to her and took Tommy from her arms. It had been a while since his niece had been this small. At first he felt awkward, holding the warm body in the bend of his elbow. The little fella's face scrunched into an unhappy look as he started to whimper. Uneasily, Joe raised the infant up onto his shoulder. No dice.

The cry increased in intensity. It was almost as if the child knew he was in unfamiliar arms. Joe didn't know what else to do but rock those arms—already feeling the burn—back and forth. Nada. The cry escalated into a full-blown scream.

"Just talk amongst yourselves," he said above the crying. "Tommy and I will take a stroll around the room. If that's okay with you," he said to the baby's mother.

She nodded. "It's you I'm worried about. He can keep this up for hours. How long can you hold out?"

"I'm tough," he said with more confidence than he felt.

He started walking around the room. The baby's ear-splitting wail slowed, but he still wouldn't quiet.

Joe stopped and instead of moving him from side to side, he commenced an up and down motion. Almost instantly the baby stopped crying. Every head in the room turned to look at him. When the quiet continued, jaws began to lower. Including Liz who stared at him as if he had two heads.

"I don't believe it," his mother said.

Neither do I, Joe wanted to chime in, but knew that would undermine his accomplishment. He wished he could take credit for the technique. But it was something he'd learned on his niece. He was glad he'd remembered. He hoped this was the final exam, the last test to show Liz that he had what it took to be in her program.

It was something he wanted to do. On top of that, as the Human Resources Director for Marchetti's, Inc., he was conducting his own unofficial research to see if on-site child care was feasible. He was always searching for forward-looking ideas to benefit the employees.

"I'm impressed, Joe," Liz said.

Was there a grudging note of respect mixed with the sincerity in her voice? He hoped so.

"Thank you," he answered, handing a dozing Tommy back to his mother.

Another baby started to fuss. Joe remembered it was the baby with the shallow latch. Valerie. Her mother, Andie, looked at him pleadingly. "Want to go for two?" she asked hopefully.

"Sure." He took the infant and tried the same technique. In a few minutes, the fussy child had calmed.

For the rest of the evening, he became the resident nanny. It gave the mothers an opportunity to listen without interruption to the group. It gave him a chance to prove something to Liz Anderson. He didn't know why that was so important to him, he only knew it was.

When time was up, the mothers all filed out and he thought their spirits were lighter than when the evening had started. Their radiant smiles as they walked past him were a big clue. So this is what a women's support group was all about, he thought. Their husbands must be grateful. He was looking forward to learning more about the program. Not to mention the intriguing and exceptionally cute Nurse Anderson.

Andie looked up at him. "Do you hire out your services?" she asked wistfully.

He shook his head. "Sorry."

"Are you going to be here next week?" Barbara asked.

"I'll have to check my schedule."

"Your social calendar?" someone asked.

"And business," he added.

Barbara smiled at him. "You would make a wonderful father, Joe. I can't believe no woman has snapped you up."

He shrugged as he looked at the group of new mothers. "All of you are already taken."

Then he was alone with Liz. She was looking at him strangely. "That was an interesting experience."

"Interesting good, or bad?" he asked crossing one ankle over the other as he leaned back against one of the gray plastic chairs.

"I'd have to say good," she answered slowly.

"You don't sound convinced. I think it was clear that they love me," he said.

"Those women are so tired they would love Godzilla if he could give them a minute-and-a-half of peace and quiet.''

''Are you comparing me to the giant lizard who ate Tokyo?''

''If the shoe fits.'' She laughed. ''I'm kidding. There's no question that you were wonderful tonight. A real hero.''

''Thank you, Ma'am.'' Before she got a chance to cancel out her compliment with a zinger, his cell phone rang. He flipped it open and said, ''Hello?''

''Joe? It's Abby.''

''Oh, geez. Abby. We had a date, didn't we?'' He smacked his forehead. He'd agreed to meet her and help her pick out a wedding present for her fiancé, his brother Nick. ''I'm about ten minutes away. I'll be there as soon as I can. Sorry, Ab. I'll make it up to you.''

''I'll hold you to that.''

He flipped the phone closed and met Liz's gaze. ''That was my sister—''

She held up her hand. ''Please don't insult my intelligence by saying that whoever called was your sister. I can't believe you forgot your date.''

''It's not a date. It's just Abby.''

''I can't believe you have so little respect for her.'' She shook her head. ''And it is a date. By definition a date is a particular time to meet someone, usually of the opposite sex.''

He nodded. ''All of that is true. But Abby is practically my sister.''

''Come on, Joe. This is me. I've already got your number. You don't have to pretend. It won't impress me. I'm immune.''

"I'm not trying to impress you. It's the truth. I'm supposed to shop with Abby for—"

"Don't. What you do on your own time is your business. The volunteer program is mine." She headed for the door. "If you fulfill that obligation, I'll be impressed."

"Liz?"

She stopped and glanced over her shoulder. "What?"

He saluted. "I will be here bright and early for orientation. I'll be the best darn cuddler you ever had."

Chapter Two

Joe held up the tiny disposable diaper and turned it over and over, eyeing it from every angle. He slid Liz a look that was part mischief, part puzzled—and one hundred percent appealing. Her heart did a little skip and she tried hard to work up a good annoyance at him for causing it. She even resurrected her feelings from the other night when he'd tried to pass off the girl on the phone as his sister. She was only marginally successful in blunting the force of her attraction.

"Even a bag of microwave popcorn has directions that say 'this side up,'" he said. "How come there's no arrow for top and bottom on this sucker?"

"A bright guy like yourself can figure it out. This is the end of orientation, the final exam. No cheating."

Liz was alone with him in the newborn nursery. He was the only trainee volunteer, darn the luck. It would have helped if other trainee volunteers were there to take the edge off the one-on-one orientation.

Liz stood beside him, next to the changing table. In front of him was a battered rag doll for practicing. She wished she could say that the green wraparound lab coat Joe wore diminished his appeal, or blurred his heartthrob image. But no such luck.

He shook his head. "You never said anything about changing diapers when you were trying to discourage me from volunteering. The term 'cuddling' seems self-explanatory and does not encompass this."

"Backing out already, Mr. Marchetti?"

"You'd like that, wouldn't you?"

"I never said I wanted you to quit."

"Not in so many words," he shot back. "But my work experience is with people. I've learned to read between the lines, decipher the body language. All the tricks of the trade."

"That's something we have in common then. I've got some people experience myself. And in mine, nine times out of ten, they'll let you down."

"Then I'll just have to show you I'm a ten," he said, giving her a boyishly mischievous look.

"Everyone needs a challenge. Mine is to make sure you can handle our little bundles of joy. The key word here is joy. You have to trust me on this. Cuddling is a more satisfying experience for everyone involved if the baby is clean and dry."

He frowned at the diaper in his hand. "Then show me the blueprint for this."

She grinned. "Sell it somewhere else. I might buy your performance if I hadn't seen Act One the other night. You know more about this baby stuff than you're letting on. The question is why you're trying to pull the wool over my eyes."

Call her a reverse chauvinist, but she found it hard

to believe that a man would volunteer to cuddle babies. Not only that, he'd shown up ten minutes ahead of schedule for his orientation. Since a part of her had expected him to let her down, she was still a little off-kilter from his early arrival.

As hard as it was to admit, Joe Marchetti was too good-looking, too charming, and too likable. She would have to be made of stone to keep from having feelings, more accurately a small, almost infinitesimal crush on the man. Her antidote—she would see his appeal and raise him a healthy dose of apathy. That meant she could neutralize the Marchetti toxin before it had a chance to work on her. She would bet her favorite stethoscope that he wasn't used to women ignoring him. But ignore him she must.

She didn't believe in happily ever after with any man, let alone a proven playboy like Mr. Marchetti. Her own father had been one. She would be a fool to fall for Joe's shtick and get dumped, or go through years of misery like her mother had. Either way her heart would come out the loser.

"Pull the wool over your eyes?" He gave her a bogus look of smarting dignity. "I'm wounded, Liz. My incentive for being here is completely above-board. One would think that *you* think I have an ulterior motive."

"Let's just say I'm skeptical." She smiled sweetly at him.

"Want to tell me why?"

She shook her head. "I want to wait and see."

He shrugged. "Suit yourself."

"After all, you signed the volunteer contract. Item one—a commitment to actively participate in the Volunteer Program, for no less than three months, three hours per week.'' She smiled and rubbed her hands together. ''That means I have you, my pretty, for the next three months—no matter what.''

''Define 'no matter what.'''

''Never you mind. Just do me proud. The life of the Cuddlers Program may be in the balance.''

''You got it.'' Then he looked at the diaper again, and the doll used for training. ''But if you ever tell anyone that I was playing with dolls, that contract won't be worth the paper I signed it on.''

''Deal,'' she said. She looked around the nursery. Empty isolettes were parked haphazardly against the wall. ''It's a slow day in here, or I would let you show off your skill with the babies.''

''You would trust me?'' he asked, phony humility in his voice.

''Now you're fishing for compliments. Like I said, the way you handled the support group babies the other night convinced me you already have a certain amount of expertise. But remember, those babies were a few weeks old. You're going to be handling little ones a couple of hours old. There's a difference.''

''Piece of cake. It's like riding a bike. You never forget.''

''You wouldn't want to share how you acquired the knowledge in the first place, would you?''

''You already know I'm an uncle.''

She nodded. ''But that doesn't qualify you for nanny of the year. I know a lot of men who want nothing to do with babies, let alone children.'' My father included, she thought before she could stop it.

''My sister Rosie strong-armed me into babysitting.''

Liz glanced from the top of his head to his worn

jeans below the hem of his lab coat, then to the tips of his scuffed loafers. He was tall and had a muscle or two tacked on to that rather attractive frame. He was no lightweight. She remembered Rosie Marchetti Schafer. Joe's little sister wasn't strong enough to force him to do anything he didn't want to. If his acquired knowledge came from babysitting his niece, it was definitely because he wanted to.

"How is your sister?" Liz asked, genuinely interested. She remembered the pretty, dark-haired woman and her hunky husband. They were hard to forget, let alone jettison the surprising envy Liz had felt watching a loving couple like Steve and Rosie Schafer.

"Fine."

Liz put a hand on her hip and shook her head at him. "I can see you didn't inherit the gift of gab."

"What?"

"Fine?" she mocked. "No embellishment? That's all you have to say?"

He stared at her for a moment, then proceeded to expertly diaper the doll without blueprints, arrows, or visual aids of any kind.

Task accomplished, he gave her his full attention. "Okay. I'll embellish. Stephanie, my niece, is beautiful, healthy and in the process of being spoiled rotten by her doting uncles and grandparents. My sister and her husband are ecstatically happy. They love being parents. They could be the poster couple for the American family."

For just a moment, Liz thought she noticed a wistful look in his eyes when he mentioned family. Then it was gone and she figured she must have imagined it. Easy to do considering where she worked.

Every day she saw moms and dads bring new

babies into the world. Some of them had other children who came to visit and welcome a new brother or sister into the family. She recalled that Joe had several brothers. The Marchettis seemed to be a large and loving clan. That didn't necessarily mean the sons were one-woman men. If nothing else, his looks made him a babe magnet. The attention he must get from women would be hard to ignore.

Not for a minute did she believe his spin from the other night. She would give anything to be able to dump her skepticism. But her childhood had been a front row seat in watching how imperfect marriage was. His parents may have stayed together for thirty-five years, but she would bet they weren't happy about it. He was just doing what playboys did. Charm a roomful of women with what he thought they wanted to hear.

She wanted to accept that he had volunteered for the reasons he'd told her the other night. But the doubting Thomas in her believed that women were nurturers who derived pleasure from holding a baby. A man who was there ostensibly for that reason had to have an ulterior motive. Either he planned to milk the experience for publicity for the family restaurant chain, or he was there to meet women. Whatever his motivation, she would do what was necessary to protect the program.

"Anything else you want to know about Rosie?" he asked.

"No. I think you've embellished sufficiently," she said sweetly.

"Good. Have *you* covered everything? About my orientation?"

She nodded. "Except which shift you want."

Just then, the nursery door opened. Samantha Taylor walked in. She was an obstetrics nurse, and a tall redhead.

"Hi, Sam," Liz said.

"Hey, boss." She glanced at Joe as if she were trying to place him, then back to Liz. "What are you doing here?"

"This is Joe Marchetti," Liz said as if that answered the question.

"Hi." Sam held out her hand. "You look familiar."

"We met about a year ago," he said shaking her hand. "My sister had her baby here."

"Yes," Sam said nodding. "Now I remember. We talked that night. I told you about the cuddlers program."

"That's right," he said, smiling that charming, orthodontia-ad smile of his.

Liz wouldn't be surprised if she'd just come face to face with the Marchetti motivation. But had Sam heard about how badly he'd used one of the other nurses? Liz wondered if she should warn her friend that he was the love 'em and leave 'em type. She couldn't blame Joe for wanting to get to know Sam better. Although signing up for the cuddlers program seemed a little extreme. Because pretty much all he had to do was stand there to make an impression on a woman.

Correction, Liz told herself, any woman but *her.*

Was it possible that she was wrong about him? Joining the cuddlers seemed like an awful lot of trouble to go through to meet a woman.

She smiled at Sam. "It seems your pitch made a

profound impression on Mr. Marchetti. He's decided to be a cuddler. I'm orienting him to the nursery."

"Ah, that explains what you're doing here on your day off," the other woman said. "I refuse to waste my breath reminding you what the word delegate means. Or explaining the downside of employee burn-out. I just came to get some money out of my purse for lunch."

Joe looked at his watch. "Is it that time already?"

Sam laughed. "I don't need a clock. My growling stomach say it's time to take a trip to the cafeteria."

"Now that you mention it, I'm hungry too," he said.

Liz had to give him credit. He'd just given himself the perfect playboy lead-in to join Sam for lunch and cast his line, work his magic, lay the groundwork for his conquest. Sam was a big girl. She could handle him. They would actually make a very attractive couple. Part of her rebelled at that thought. The other part was glad that he would show his true colors and be out of there before anyone learned to depend on him.

"Good," Liz said. "Sam can give you an impromptu tour of the hospital on the way."

"On the way where?" he asked, looking puzzled.

"To the cafeteria."

"You in a hurry to get rid of me?" One dark eyebrow rose questioningly.

Sam cleared her throat. "If she's not, she should be."

Joe looked at her a moment, then chuckled. "I'm going to assume you didn't mean that the way it came out."

"I didn't." She looked sheepish. "What I meant was that this woman spends too much time here—six days a week on average. Last I heard she wasn't supposed to come in today."

"A workaholic dedicated to showing one volunteer the ropes," Joe said, shaking his head. "This is all my fault."

"No. There's always something," Liz said. "So I'll leave you two to the rest of the tour—" She gasped when Joe took her elbow and headed her toward the door.

He looked over his shoulder and said to a grinning Sam, "Nice to meet you. Don't let me keep you from your lunch. I'm sure I can find out where you hide the cafeteria another time. After ruining her day off, I owe this lady some R and R. Bye."

Thirty minutes after leaving the Encino hospital Joe parked his convertible in a beach lot overlooking the Pacific Ocean. There were picnic tables scattered in the sand nearby. He half turned to look at Liz. Her hair curled charmingly around her small face. A becoming pink colored her cheeks. Sunglasses hid the keen intelligence in her eyes. But what really drew his attention was her smile. A rare phenomenon he was beginning to realize. And that was a shame. Because it was very attractive and incredibly appealing.

He was only slightly miffed that driving with the top down had produced the occurrence and not his own witty repartee. No matter. He planned to bring it out more frequently. Everyone needed a challenge. Even a confirmed bachelor like himself.

"This is the spot I was telling you about," he said.

She sighed. "I can't remember the last time I drove to the beach."

He grabbed the brown bag with the sandwiches

he'd bought at a stand on Pacific Coast Highway and got out of the car. Rounding it, he opened the passenger door and took the cardboard container of drinks that Liz had been holding on her lap.

"Let's sit on one of those benches over there," he said pointing. "Great scenery."

She nodded and slid out. They walked to the picnic table and she clambered over the bench, settling herself to face the ocean. Joe never missed a chance at that view. This time it was a perfect excuse to sit beside her, his arm brushing her shoulder. She shivered slightly, then shifted a bit to the side.

"You cold?" he asked.

"Nope." She shook her head. "Not after Mr. Toad's Wild Ride in that car with the top down. And I meant that in a good way."

"Which part? The wild ride? Or Mr. Toad?" he asked wryly.

"Let me just say, nice car. Really, really nice," she finished, glancing over her shoulder to look at it with an exaggerated sigh.

Joe loved his sporty red convertible. But he couldn't tell whether she really meant what she'd said, or if there was subtle criticism in her voice.

"I like it," he said cautiously.

She peeked over her shoulder again. "No back seat. That's good news and bad."

"How's that?" he asked. He liked the fact that Liz kept him on his toes, always wondering what she would say. What zinger would she lob his way? And how would he defend himself?

"Well, the good news is that car is a babe magnet."

"If one were looking to attract 'babes.'"

She studied him. "Isn't that what playboys do?"

There was the zinger. And he suspected his best defense was offhandedness. "I wouldn't know."

"Well if you didn't write the whole thing, I'd bet you contributed at least a chapter to the how-to book for bachelors on the make."

On the make? Defending himself for something he'd done was one thing. But she had him all wrong. For some reason he didn't have a clue about, she'd pegged him in a negative light from the day he'd walked into her office. It was time to find out what had tied her stethoscope in a knot.

"And why would you think that?" he asked.

"You fit the profile."

"What does that mean?"

"You're good-looking, smart, and you have a great job."

"Thank you."

"Observation, not compliment." She sipped her soda. "Those attributes are a triple whammy. Women must swarm all over you."

"You make me sound like the bait for a roach motel."

She laughed. "Just remember the insect image is yours, not mine. But seriously, you would have to be stupid not to play the field."

If she was bitchy or nasty, he could get mad and fight down and dirty. But her manner was conversational. Light and breezy. This was one for the books—Nurse Ratchett with overtones of Tinkerbell. Her good nature was infectious even while she was tossing verbal barbs his way. She'd lobbed him so many backhanded compliments, he felt like a tennis player. How could he defend himself against that?

He took a bite of his sandwich and chewed thoughtfully. "I suppose you could describe me as relationship challenged," he said. "I prefer that to stupid."

"So being relationship challenged has set in since Trish Hudson?"

Joe remembered his short acquaintance with the nurse. Something about her had put him off and he'd ended things with her in a straightforward way. "What about her?"

"Didn't you date?"

"We went out a couple times," he answered carefully.

"What happened?" Liz seemed tense, as if she was ready to pounce on his response.

He was no stranger to the need for diplomacy in employee relations. Liz and Trish worked in the same hospital. Just because he'd ended things on account of the negative vibes she'd given off, there was no need to spread that to her co-workers. "Things just didn't work out," he finally said.

"So that's what you call it?" she asked, an edge to her voice.

"What?" he asked, honestly at a loss.

"Never mind." She stared at the water for a few moments before asking, "Relationship challenged? Does that mean you don't fool around?" she asked skeptically.

"I used to. Not anymore."

"And you don't flirt?"

"Flirt is a relative term. I'm a people person. Friendly. It's a management style. An asset for the Human Resources Director of Marchetti's, Inc."

"There are assets, and then there are assets. In your

position, you get to scope out the territory right off the bat.''

''What does that mean?'' he asked sharply.

''You can check out every new female employee.''

''Red light,'' he said, shaking his head. ''No way. It's my job to make sure that kind of thing *doesn't* happen. We stop short of restricting employee fraternization. But it's strongly discouraged.''

''That could explain why you're a volunteer.''

He wondered what she meant by that—nothing good probably. Watching her for a moment, he tried to figure out why he cared whether or not she thought badly of him.

Tamping down his annoyance he said, ''Does the phrase 'Don't judge a book by its cover' mean anything to you?''

''Have you ever heard 'if it looks like a duck, walks like a duck and quacks like a duck, it must be a duck'?'' He stared at her for a few moments and she said, ''What?''

''I'm just trying to figure out when I quacked or waddled. What behavior have I exhibited to make you think so poorly of me?''

''The very first time I met you, you were trying to impress me with your charm.''

''And you nearly ripped my ear off. Apparently my technique could use some fine tuning. Or I need a brush-up course.''

She shook her head. ''Don't waste your time on my account. I'm immune.''

No kidding, he thought. The question was why?

He wiped his hands on a napkin. ''Turnabout is fair play and I've been getting a grilling that would do the CIA proud. Let me ask you something.''

"Fair enough. Shoot," she said, chewing contentedly.

"How long have you been divorced?"

She almost choked. "What makes you think that?"

"You have a chip on your shoulder the size of Texas. You camouflage it pretty well with humor. But you've got some baggage, lady."

Her eyes widened, and he expected her to dispute his words. But she only said, "Thankfully it wasn't a nasty divorce. One would have to be married first." She fiddled with her sandwich wrapping. "I'm proud to say, I've never had that pleasure. I'm single and satisfied and plan to stay that way."

"Then someone dumped on you."

"You think? What was your first clue?"

"Because you're wary. Of men. You don't get that way without some help. And I'm paying the price for what some other guy did."

He knew he'd hit close to the mark when she looked away. Watching her profile, he could see her jaw clench.

"I'm not wary of men," she finally said. "I just have a problem with the ones who don't play by the rules."

"And you think I fall into that category?"

"The first time we met you threatened to pick me up bodily and lock me in the broom closet. If I recall correctly, your exact words were that visiting hours were for everyone but you."

"I was kidding about the broom closet."

"I know. But not about breaking the rules."

"Cut me some slack, Nurse Ratchett. My baby sister had just had a baby. First one in the family. I wanted to spend some time with her."

"And you think you're the only new uncle who feels that way? Picture what would happen if everyone acted the way you did."

"The obstetrics wing would be full of lots of happy uncles."

"Probably. Followed quickly by anarchy and chaos." She shook her head. "Not on my watch. Mothers and babies at risk? Completely unacceptable. It's my job to keep order."

Joe couldn't help admiring the fact that she took her job seriously. Protecting new mothers and babies. Patients in her care were lucky. He had a feeling anyone she cared about would be lucky. But there was a protective shield around her, emotionally speaking, and he wondered why she worked so hard at keeping it in place.

"The fact that I'm volunteering at the hospital does nothing to alter your opinion of me?"

"It would if I didn't get the feeling that on the heels of your good deed was a rule waiting to be broken. Or a skirt waiting to be chased, so to speak."

"Why would you think that?"

"By the time I'd met you twice, you were coming on to three different women." She held up her hand and started counting on her fingers. "There was the blonde I saw you with when you visited your sister in the hospital, Trish Hudson, and Abby, the woman you practically stood up because you got sidetracked scoping out the volunteer program."

"Have you ever heard the phrase 'benefit of the doubt'?" he asked wryly.

"Yes. But I can't help feeling that you don't know the meaning of the word longevity or sincerity. And your heart is a revolving door. I'm sorry, but based on what I've seen it's hard for me to believe your motivation is anything but self-serving.''

Joe considered himself a pretty easygoing guy. From the moment he'd walked into her office, he'd taken it in the shorts from Nurse Ratchett without fighting back. No more Mr. Nice Guy. It was time to set the record straight.

He rolled his sandwich wrapping into a ball and tossed it into a nearby trash can. Then he turned to Liz.

''All right,'' he said seriously. ''You win. I'll tell you my ulterior motive.''

Chapter Three

Liz couldn't believe she'd heard him right. "You're going to tell the truth?"

"Yeah."

Blow his cover? Come clean so soon? She couldn't imagine why he would do that. But then what harm could it do? No doubt there were females at the hospital just as anxious to meet him as he was to meet them. She only wanted honesty from him. Although for some men that was too much to ask.

But what if she was wrong? What if he'd already told her the truth? His motivation *might* have something to do with wanting to help. But he wouldn't turn his back on the opportunity to meet a woman. After all, Sam had given him the speech about the program.

"It's Samantha, isn't it?" she asked.

"Samantha?"

"She's a tall redhead. It's understandable that you would want to get to know her better. Although why you'd go to all the trouble of volunteering is beyond me. A simple phone call would suffice. As a matter of fact, why didn't you take *her* to lunch? You're slipping, Slick. Missed a golden opportunity there—''

She realized he hadn't said a word. He was just watching her run off at the mouth.

''Are you finished?'' he asked.

''I can be.''

''Good. Because you're way off base.''

''Am I?'' she asked warily.

''Number one, I genuinely want to give a little time to the hospital as a volunteer for the reasons I told you. And for the fact that my sister and my niece received wonderful care. Not to mention my grandmother when she was there for tests.''

''Okay, if you say so.''

''Number two, and here's the good part.''

He half turned toward her looking intensely serious, which was very cute. But he also had an earnest expression, so full of an emotion she'd accused him of not having—sincerity. It nearly convinced her that he would tell her the truth.

''I've been thinking about something for a while,'' he said. ''And this is work related.''

''What?'' she asked, sipping her soda.

''On-site child care for restaurant employees in every location.''

He looked dead serious. She stared at him. ''Say again.''

''It's my job to be a liaison between management and the employees. To me there's more involved than staffing and monitoring benefits. One of the biggest problems I see is child care. Finding reliable, affordable, trustworthy help is tough.''

"You could have hired a company to check this out for you."

He shook his head. "Marchetti's is a family-owned business. A good part of our success is directly related to hands-on managing. This is my 'baby.' Pardon the pun."

Liz took off her sunglasses and looked at him. Was it possible that her first impression of Joe Marchetti was wrong? Could it be that he wasn't the shallow philanderer she'd taken him for? But what about Trish and the way he'd used her?

"What do you hope to accomplish by observing a hospital newborn nursery?" she asked.

"For one thing, it will give me some idea whether or not on-site care is feasible for infants. I'm not sure we can provide that much help."

"But it's such an important stage."

"I know. It's a bonding time for mothers and babies."

"You've done your homework." When the compliment earned her an attractive grin, her heart skipped a beat. But she managed another question. "So what happens after you critique our facility?"

Liz found that she was warming to the idea. Even if he was fabricating the whole thing, the fact that he had given the subject so much thought elevated him in her eyes.

"I need to observe different child-care environments to see if we can furnish adequate attention for such a broad age range. Once they start kindergarten, the parents have more choices. Schools have programs in place for supervision."

She shook her head in disbelief. "Wow."

"What?"

"You really *have* done your homework. This is an important issue. Not just for your company, but everywhere. With the economic climate what it is, very often it takes two paychecks to support a family."

He nodded thoughtfully. "A high percentage of our employees are women. The lucky ones have family to look after the kids. But we lose way too many skilled and dedicated workers because they can't find dependable, affordable nurturing people to watch their children. I already told you about my secretary."

She nodded. "We have the same problem at the hospital."

"It's a domino effect. The babysitter doesn't show up. Someone doesn't come to work because they can't leave their children unattended. I sympathize, but I have a business to run." He studied her a moment. "In your business inadequate staffing could mean life and death."

"A long shot. But, worst case scenario, definitely possible," she agreed.

In his enthusiasm he angled his body toward her, causing their legs to brush. The contact sent a wave of warmth crashing through her. His excitement wasn't all she'd noticed. And his boyish appeal was making it harder not to go there—to that place where she *liked* him. Before she could do that there had to be trust. That wasn't going to happen.

"I've been reading up on the pros as well as the cons of child care," he said.

"What have you found?" she asked, pleased that her voice sounded relatively normal.

"Leaving a baby or young child with someone other than a parent doesn't have to be a negative. They can learn to interact with people other than their parents in a positive way. Very often other adults have something to offer a child that can make them a more well-rounded individual. They become accustomed to others and less shy.''

"I'm impressed, Joe.''

"Really?''

His pleased smile set off a chain reaction within her that was one part fear, three parts surrender. This was unacceptable.

"You bet,'' she said. "When you set out to do something, you really scope out your objective.''

His grin slipped. "What does that mean?''

"Whatever your real purpose for volunteering, you've put major time and effort into it. Most guys aren't so imaginative. 'What's your sign' is as creative as they get.''

As soon as the words were out she wanted to call them back. He didn't deserve that.

"Now I see.''

She didn't know what he saw, but it didn't make him want to do the dance of joy. Her words had extinguished the warmth and passionate animation from his eyes. The coldness there made her shiver. It also made her sad. Just a moment ago his lips were smiling and full—so much so that she couldn't help wondering if they would be warm and soft against her own. Now his mouth pulled tight. Tense. Angry.

"What's wrong?'' she asked.

"You still think I'm on the make.''

She didn't bother to deny it. Game playing wasn't her style. She'd learned to hate it. "It's a reasonable assumption.''

"Because I'm single, good-looking and I have a

great job." His voice was even deeper than usual, with an edge that clued her in to his annoyance.

"You're the complete opposite of our customary volunteer. If you were in my position, wouldn't you be skeptical?"

He let out a long breath. "For the record, I'm not interested in dating. I gave it up. It's an exercise in futility. And a colossal waste of time. I have better things to do than spend awkward evenings with someone only to find out it will never amount to anything."

He looked awfully sincere. There was that word again. Liz wondered if she should give him the benefit of the doubt. She shook her head. Even if all the evidence wasn't stacked against him, she couldn't let herself believe. It was too hard when she was wrong.

Liz stood. "The bottom line is that what *I* think about you doesn't matter. You've signed up to volunteer in my program. As long as you show up for your shift and conduct yourself in a manner that won't jeopardize the babies or the program, whatever else you do is irrelevant to me."

"Fair enough," he said, standing, too. "If you're finished eating, I'll take you back to the hospital now."

Oddly enough she didn't want to go back to the hospital. But it was probably for the best, Liz thought a little sadly.

"What are you doing here, Joe?" Flo Marchetti looked at her second son as if he had two heads.

"I can't stop by to say hello to my favorite mother?" He leaned over and kissed her cheek.

She stood and turned her back on the flat of plants

as she removed her gardening gloves. She was tall, silver-haired, and he couldn't help thinking the years had been kind to her. She was still a very attractive woman and he understood how she'd kept his father interested for so many years. That thought gave him an odd feeling, as if something bad had happened, something he couldn't quite put his finger on. Weird, he thought, shaking his head to dispel the sensation.

Sliding her sunglasses to the top of her head, Flo peered intently at him. "What's your problem?"

Brunette. About five foot two, one-hundred-and-five pounds, hazel eyes. Name Elizabeth Anderson. But that wasn't for general publication. His run-in with her had made him edgy and restless—he hadn't been able to face his empty condo. So he'd stopped by to see the folks.

"Where's Dad?" he asked, glancing toward the house.

"Golfing with Nick and Steve. They called you for a foursome, but you weren't home. Where have you been?"

Orienting for the cuddlers program. Something else he didn't want to put out for general publication. So he just said, "Driving. To the beach."

"Girl trouble." She clucked sympathetically.

So much for keeping secrets from his mother. "For Pete's sake, Ma. Why do you jump to that conclusion based on what I just told you?"

"I'm right. You asked a question instead of denying it. I'm glad."

"That I have girl trouble?"

"See?" She pointed her gardening trowel at him. "I knew I was right."

"That's not what I said. I can't believe you're so happy that I could have problems."

"Relationship concerns. There's a difference."

"And you think that I have a problem with a woman?" He would go to his grave without telling her she was right.

"I know so. And I'm not happy about it. Not exactly," she added.

"What does that mean?"

She sat down on the lounge beside the pool and motioned for him to sit on the matching chaise across from her. "You're my son. I love you. I'd scratch out the eyes of any woman who hurt you. But—"

"Go on," he prompted. He was going to be sorry for this, he knew. But for some reason he needed to hear what she had to say.

"Well, you're not getting any younger. Nice—unattached—girls in your age group are getting harder to find."

He thought about Liz, the fact that she'd never married. And, as his mother so bluntly put it, she was in the appropriate age bracket. Which meant she wasn't getting any younger either.

"I'm not looking, Ma."

"Good."

"Good?" he asked, puzzled. "That's not some kind of reverse psychology stuff, is it?"

"Of course not. That would never work on you. It simply means that when you're not looking for it, love is more likely to find you."

"No really. I mean it. I have no intention of getting serious about anyone."

"And why's that?" she asked.

"You and Dad."

"What about your father and I?" she asked sharply.

He stared at her. Her reaction seemed out of proportion to his comment. "I just meant you two are so perfect together. I wouldn't want to make a mistake."

"Everyone makes mistakes, dear. It's not the end of the world. You have to get over that." She looked at him. "Rosie took the marriage plunge. And Nick found Abby right under his nose. They would be married now if she wasn't so set on a June wedding. In a few weeks Abby will be Mrs. Nick Marchetti." She sighed. "I can't wait for the wedding. Do you have a date yet?"

She was like a bloodhound, focused on the scent of her prey. He shook his head. "Ma, don't you ever get tired of meddling?"

Flo sighed as she shook her head. "You don't have a date. I hate to be the one to tell you this, Joey. But you can't wait much longer. You'll be too old to, you know—do the wild thing."

There was that "you know" again. He preferred that euphemism to his mother's. If that's what this was all about, it would be easy. Liz was right about women throwing themselves at him. But he was looking for—what? The perfect woman? He knew she didn't exist. A perfect relationship? Ditto.

"Ma, it's just not as easy now as it was when you and Dad got hitched."

"You think it was easy then?" she asked. There was that unfamiliar sharpness in her tone again.

"For you and Dad? Yeah." He ran a hand through his hair. "Almost everyone I know from high school has been married and divorced at least once. Some more than that. I see single mothers every day, struggling to keep it together. Not to mention the dads paying child support and seeing their kids every other weekend.'' He shook his head. ''Not me. I've decided to stay unattached rather than wind up a statistic of failure.''

''One thing never changes. If you want something to be successful, you work at it. You don't give up.''

''Or don't try at all.''

She pointed her trowel at him again. ''I didn't raise cowards, Joseph Paul Marchetti.''

Uh oh. When she used all three of his names, it was time to change the subject.

''So when did the guys decide to go golfing?''

''This morning. That reminds me. Where were you so early?''

For some reason, he didn't want her or anyone to know about the cuddling program. She would start matchmaking—jumping to wrong conclusions. Not unlike a certain cute nurse he was trying to get out of his mind. And if his brothers found out, there would be no peace. It was best to keep this to himself.

''I guess I just didn't hear the phone,'' he said vaguely.

''Haven't you heard? There's this handy little invention called an answering machine.''

He grinned. ''I've heard of it, Ma.''

''I should hope so.'' She snapped her fingers. ''That reminds me of something else. Your niece's first birthday party is going to be here at the house in a few weeks. You will show up?''

He decided not to ask why a phone machine would make his mother think of Stephanie's birthday. One short year ago she'd come into this world and brightened their lives. Steve was a lucky man. A *family* man. Remembering that day brought him an image of Liz Anderson.

After his anger from their encounter had subsided, he'd realized that in all probability she hadn't been born cynical. Something had happened to make her that way. He intended to find out what that something was.

"I wouldn't miss my niece's birthday. You can count on me."

"With a date?"

"Don't push it, Ma."

At 4:32 a.m. Liz wheeled the isolette down the hall to the nursery. She was tired after a long night. Her mind flashed onto the conversation she'd had a few days before with Joe Marchetti. About employees not showing up for work. It had happened tonight. It was her job to plug up the holes in the schedule. Hence her being there when sane people were sleeping.

Sane adults, she amended. There were an awful lot of births in the wee hours of the morning. Like this sweet little girl, she thought smiling. A textbook delivery. Her mother was resting comfortably. The family pediatrician had checked out the new arrival who was now peacefully slumbering after her traumatic ordeal.

Liz wheeled her into the nursery and parked the isolette beside an empty one. She leaned over the tiny newborn and smiled again. "It doesn't seem fair, little one. For nine months life is good. Then, bam. You make your entrance into the world and your dignity is stripped away. I promise it gets better, princess."

"Do you know that from personal experience?"

Liz whirled at the sound of the familiar deep voice. Joe. "What are you doing here?"

"I could ask you the same question."

"I work here." And until now working successfully at avoiding you, she silently added.

"I volunteer here," he said.

She knew that too. For the last few weeks, he'd kept his promise and shown up for the 6:00 p.m. to 9:00 p.m. cuddler shift. Sometimes he worked more than once a week. She'd made a point of reading the volunteer sign-in sheet, just to check up on him.

"So I see. Why so early?" she asked, shaking her head. "Let me rephrase. It's not early. It's practically the middle of the night. Are you crazy?"

"I know this isn't the customary time," was all he said.

"That's it?" She shook her head. "You have an annoying habit of not embellishing."

He shrugged. "I'm a man of few words."

Who apparently didn't need a lot of sleep, she thought. He confidently held the infant in his arms as he sat in the rocking chair. His cheeks and jaw were smudged with whiskers. His dark hair was rumpled as if he'd just rolled out of bed. A visual that did strange things to her insides.

"This isn't the shift you agreed to. Breaking the rules already, I see," she teased, mildly surprised that she bore him no ill will. But it was darn near impossible to work up a good mad at a hunky guy holding a newborn baby.

"The night security officer let me in," he offered.

"I'm not questioning your method. Just your timing. It's four in the morning. Shouldn't you be getting your beauty sleep?"

"No." He met her gaze. "And since when do you work this shift?"

She'd just been thinking the average adult should be sleeping and only the batty ones were up and about. Apparently she and Joe both needed to take a sanity pill.

"I fill in where necessary," she said with a shrug.

Two could play their cards close to the vest. He wasn't talking about why he was there so early. She sure as shootin' wasn't going to give him the satisfaction of revealing that she had done it a lot lately. Mostly to avoid watching him trifle with female hearts.

But even a cynic like herself couldn't help noticing that 4:30 a.m. wasn't the most favorable flirting time. The majority of the staff on this shift had specific reasons for working it. Primarily children. A two-income household could easily split child care responsibilities this way.

Joe shifted his position in the rocker. "The hospital is lucky to have someone so dedicated."

The compliment warmed her. "Thanks. I think of it the other way around. I'm grateful to have them." She angled her head toward the bundle he was holding. "She's a beauty isn't she?"

He glanced down and smiled, a tender look that tugged at Liz's heart. "Yeah," he said.

"Boggles the mind, doesn't it? Life is a blank slate for this little girl. She has to learn to walk, talk—everything."

Joe looked at her. "It's hard to believe that one short year ago my niece was about this size. Now she's walking."

"Is she?" Liz was genuinely interested.

He nodded. "It's amazing how much ground she covers with her short, pudgy legs."

"That's great." Liz smiled a little wistfully. "The one drawback about this job is that we send the babies home and most we never see again. As the support group moms get a handle on things, they disappear, busy with their lives. I'd love to get periodic updates on the kids."

Joe studied her for a moment. "So come to her birthday party."

"What? Who?"

"My niece. It's this Saturday. At my folks because they've got the biggest house with the most toys—swimming pool, table tennis etcetera. And there's room for the whole family. It's going to be an outdoor thing in the backyard. Very informal."

"I don't know—"

"My brothers will be there—"

"Ah, now I get it."

"What?"

"You want to finish the job you started a year ago. Locking me in the broom closet. And that's supposed to make me want to come?"

He chuckled softly. "I promise there are no closets with locks anywhere on the premises." He settled the baby more comfortably in his arms.

Liz remembered his brothers. All the Marchetti men were exceptionally good-looking. Although she thought Joe the most handsome. From a strictly observational point of view. They had made her laugh. And their love and loyalty and protectiveness on behalf of little sister Rosie was very appealing. A big devoted family. If nothing else, she wanted to see what that was like. Find out if such a thing really existed. In her experience it was the stuff of fantasy and fairy tales.

"In that case, I'd be delighted to go," she agreed.

He looked momentarily surprised, but recovered quickly and simply said, "Good."

Several hours later Liz walked down the hall. It was time for the changing of the guard. The day shift nurses came on about fifteen minutes before starting work to take reports from the departing night personnel. The volunteer sign-in book was on the counter beside the timeclock. Joe was there, standing head and shoulders above several women surrounding him.

Liz felt her stomach knot. Just when she was beginning to believe that she'd been wrong about him, the sight of him and his acquired harem hit her between the eyes. And the worst part was that they were all women she liked and respected.

At least it explained why he'd been in the nursery during the night. This was the group of women that he hadn't scoped out yet. Catch the first shift just as they came on duty, while they were fresh. Even as that catty thought raced through her mind, she dismissed it. That was way too much effort for a playboy. But if that wasn't his angle, what was he doing there in the middle of the night?

As she drew closer, she spotted Samantha and heard her say, "I'm looking forward to the weekend. Almost every Saturday we have a weekly unwinding session."

"It's cool," said Jeannie Drummond. She was a plump brunette, fun and witty. "Just dinner. But there are always laughs. We pick a place where anyone who wants to can dance. You should join us, Joe."

In her enthusiasm, perky blonde Tanya Quinn grabbed his arm. "Great idea. Come on, Joe. It'll be fun."

As the conversation wafted over to Liz, her spirits deflated like a punctured balloon. She hadn't realized until that moment how much his invitation had pumped her. So much for meeting his family on Saturday, she thought. What philanderer in his right mind would pass up playboy heaven to go to a family gathering? Although she believed he was fond of his niece, it was a child's birthday party.

After searching so hard for it, she'd finally found confirmation for what she'd always believed to be his ulterior motive. Yet she took no satisfaction in being right. She felt angry—and sad.

"Sounds like you ladies know how to have a good time," he said.

"We sure do," Jeannie agreed. "Say you'll come. All work and no play, and all that—"

"Studies have proven that time off for the work force is necessary to recharge their batteries. You need to let your hair down," he said.

"So we'll see you there?" Tanya asked.

He shook his head. "Sorry. I can't make it. But you ladies have a good time. See you next week."

He extricated himself from Tanya's grip while Liz was—metaphorically speaking—lifting her chin off the floor. He had turned them down! Flat. If she hadn't heard with her own ears, she wouldn't have believed it.

She watched him toss the group a farewell wave. Then he walked toward her with a smile on his face that turned her legs to noodles and her heart to a bongo drum.

He stopped and looked down at her. "You're just the person I was looking for."

"Oh?" A darned intelligent response, she thought. Especially when her mind had turned into oatmeal.

"I wanted to let you know that I'll call you and arrange to pick you up for the party at my folks." He started moving again. "I'd do it now, but I'm late. Gotta get ready for work. Bye," he said with a grin and a wave.

Then he was gone. Before her off-the-scale pulse returned to normal. Before she could say sorry I misjudged you. Or check his forehead for fever. He'd passed up an invitation from three women to see his family, and her!

She firmly shook her head. This wasn't about her. He was just giving her an opportunity to see his niece. And she wanted to see him interact with his family. Because that would give her some insight into what made Joe Marchetti tick. She could be wrong about him. And it was very important *not* to be wrong. She wasn't sure why, but she had to know if he was one of the good guys.

Chapter Four

Joe read the look of terror on Liz's face as she gaped at his parents' house and all the cars parked out front. He hadn't thought the spunky nurse was afraid of anything. Especially his family. Interesting to find this chink in her starched white cap. Sort of endearing— as if she needed him. Until now, she'd always acted as if she didn't need anyone. Particularly a man.

"The house really isn't as big as it looks. Sort of an optical illusion," he said as they walked to the door.

"Okay."

From the moment he'd plopped his volunteer form down on her desk, he'd been focused on improving her low opinion of him. Now that he'd managed to get her to spend some time in his company, he wasn't sure how he felt about it or what to do with her.

"Just stick close to me. I won't let anything happen to you," he said.

"Okay." But she continued to stare at the big house and yuppie cars.

As he looked down at her, the way the sun brought out the red highlights in her pixie cut hair and made the roses in her cheeks bloom, the idea of her *real* close to him hiked up his heart rate. He couldn't remember the last time, if ever, a woman had prompted such poetic thoughts in him.

His supportive words didn't seem to fill her with confidence, so he decided a win-one-for-the-Gipper speech was in order. "Don't be scared. I promise this won't hurt a bit."

"That's my line. And more often than not I'm lying through my teeth." Liz swallowed hard as she clutched the birthday-gift bag she held. "I thought you said this was a family party."

"It is," he agreed. "But you remember I have brothers." He saw her nod. "They're all here." He scanned the line of cars in a semicircle on the curved driveway. "Correction. They're all here but Nick."

"It's a little overwhelming for someone who grew up an only child."

"I can't imagine what that must have been like," he said as they stepped onto the porch. "But I'd like to hear about it. I'd like to get to know you better."

Liz shook her head. "No you wouldn't. Boring."

"I doubt that," he answered. Nothing about her was boring.

Especially the way she looked. He noted her white canvas tennis shoes and red T-shirt tucked into white shorts. When he'd finally gotten hold of her at work to find out where she lived, he'd told her to dress cool and casual because the party was going to be on the patio and the weather rumor was for a May heat wave.

The way that shirt outlined her breasts and disappeared into the small waistband of her white shorts accentuating her curvy hips—well it was more than a rumor that his temperature had climbed a degree or two higher in the blink of an eye and continued to shoot up.

Before he could dwell on that any longer, he opened the door and listened. "It's too quiet. They must be on the patio," he said.

He led the way through the house. When he glanced over his shoulder and found her missing, he retraced his steps and found her admiring the family room.

"This room is bigger than the apartment I grew up in," she said. "Do I need to leave a trail of crumbs to find my way out?"

"Just send up a flare and someone will rescue you."

"Okay." She shook her head in awe. "The furniture is beautiful. I love the floral sofas and that shade of beige carpet," she said. "This house is wonderful."

"Wait till you see the backyard."

He grabbed her hand, just so he didn't lose her again, he told himself. Certainly not because he was trying to keep her close. But he felt pretty good when she didn't pull away. They walked through the dining room and kitchen, then out the back door onto the brick patio.

"Hi, everyone," he said raising his hand in a wave.

"Joey." His mother got up from the glass-topped patio table and walked over to them. She gave him a hug, then smiled warmly at Liz.

"Ma, this is my friend, Liz Anderson. She works at the hospital where Rosie had Stephanie."

"I remember," Flo said. "You're practically a legend in this family the way you took care of Joe."

"It was nothing," Liz said with a grin.

"Don't encourage her, Ma. Liz and I ran into each other and she said she never gets to see the babies when they go home so I invited her to the party."

"Florence Marchetti," his mother said smiling warmly as she shook Liz's hand.

"It's a pleasure to see you again, Mrs. Marchetti," Liz answered.

"Flo please. And that's Joe's father, Tom. There's the birthday girl digging in my garden," she said ruefully.

Joe saw his niece with her father hovering close by, laughing as she filled her chubby fists with dirt and tossed it in the air.

"The last time I saw her," Liz said, "she was so tiny. Just look at her now. All that dark hair. And those wonderful curls. She's adorable."

"Please don't look at her until I get her cleaned up." Rosie had opened the door behind them just in time to hear what Liz said. She came out with a washcloth in her hand. "Hi, Liz." His sister's smile of greeting was genuinely friendly.

"Hi, Rosie," Liz answered.

"Obviously you two need no introduction," Joe said to his sister.

"She's one unforgettable nurse. It's not every day a woman her size can bounce you out of a hospital room. My hat's off to you."

"You, too?" Joe said. "My whole family is turning against me."

Ignoring him, Rosie said, "It's nice to see you again, Liz."

"Same here," Liz said laughing. "It looks as if we'll be seeing you in my neck of the hospital woods pretty soon."

Ruefully, Rosie looked down at her rounded belly. "It can't be too soon for me. But I have four more weeks and the doctor seems to think I'm going all the way to term."

"I hope I'm on duty when you come in."

"Me, too."

Joe hoped so too. Her dedication to mothers and babies meant that his little sister and the new baby would be in good hands. He pointed to the two ruffians playing paddle tennis. "You remember them. Tweedledumb and Tweedledumber. Alex and Luke."

"Which is which?" Liz asked.

"Alex is taller," Rosie said. "Excuse me. I need to figure out some way to convince my daughter that dirt isn't a toy and it needs to stay in Grandma's garden." She looked ruefully at the washcloth in her hand. "And I think this will do more harm than good. We need a bath."

"Good luck," Liz said. "She's having such a wonderful time."

Rosie sighed. "I may need your help, Uncle Joe. No one except her father can distract her as well as you."

He grinned down at Liz. "I swear I didn't put her up to singing my praises."

"Yeah. And I bet you've got oceanfront property for sale in Arizona," she teased.

Joe knew she was kidding. At this particular moment. But only because Rosie's remark had obviously been spontaneous. He knew she was still wary, but he had a plan. Before the day was over, she would know for a fact that he was a nice guy.

When his niece let out a piercing wail, he put his Liz problem on a back burner. For the next several minutes, he practically stood on his head to keep Stephanie happy and unaware that they were coaxing her away from dirt—mother nature's plaything. When he spotted Liz again, he noticed Alex and Luke had put their paddle tennis game aside to talk to her. He frowned at the threesome. She was laughing at something Alex had said.

If he had a jealous bone in his body he would be tempted to challenge either or both of them to paddles at twenty paces for the way they hovered around Liz. But one had to be emotionally engaged for the jealousy thing to happen. That was the furthest thing from his mind. Since he was convinced there was no such phenomenon as Ms. Right. And failure wasn't an option for him. He'd seen too many shattered dreams, too many friends who vowed never to say "I do" again because of a painful divorce, too many lives changed for the worse after a walk down the aisle. Nope. He believed that single plus single equaled serene.

He walked over to the threesome. "Are they behaving?" he asked Liz.

"Perfectly," she said.

"That would be a first." He hoped no one heard the edge in his voice.

No such luck he realized when Luke whistled. He didn't say anything, proving that he was a class act. But Joe didn't miss the questioning look in his brother's eyes. Not to mention a wry expression that said he'd made his own assessment of what was going on.

Joe planned to set him straight when they were alone. Right now he tried to analyze his problem. He thought he'd just talked himself *out* of attitude. Not only that, he knew neither of his brothers would ever move in on a woman he'd brought. So what had made him take even a subtle verbal shot?

His only excuse was that he'd worked damn hard and long to even begin to thaw Liz out where he was concerned. She'd known his brothers all of ten minutes, not counting that time in Rosie's hospital room, and she acted like she would trust them with her firstborn. Why was she standoffish only with him?

He was about to steer her aside and ask when the kitchen door opened again and Nick arrived with his fiancée. Out walked his plan to prove to Liz that he was a straight arrow, a salt-of-the-earth kind of guy. Joe couldn't wait for Liz to meet them. After the two lovebirds made their rounds of the family, he motioned his brother over to where he stood beside Liz.

Joe cleared his throat. "Liz Anderson, I'd like you to meet my brother Nick and his fiancée, *Abby.*"

Joe stared at Liz, waiting for her reaction. He wasn't disappointed. Her eyes opened wide and the color in her cheeks deepened to a becoming pink. Her smile faltered and when he met her gaze, she quickly looked away.

She shook hands with both of them. "It's a pleasure to meet you."

"Same here," Nick said, slipping his arm around Abby's waist. She briefly rested her blond head on his shoulder, snuggling into the embrace.

Lucky son of a gun, Joe couldn't help thinking. The

thought was brief, but the stab of envy was much longer and sharper. They made a terrific-looking couple. Nick's tall, dark good looks were an attractive counterpoint to Abby's petite, blond prettiness. Nick deserved someone as sweet and loyal as Abby. It had taken him quite a while to get over a particularly nasty rejection. When he had, he and Abby had fallen in love.

"In a few weeks, Abby's going to be my *sister,*" Joe said. He knew it was a low blow, but he couldn't help emphasizing the last word after she'd raked him over the coals.

Liz's full lips turned up slightly in a wan smile. "Is that so?"

Abby's blue eyes sparkled with happiness. "Can't be soon enough for me. Not only do I get the best guy in the world, but I also get to be a part of the best family in the world." Her brow wrinkled thoughtfully. "Joe, did I thank you for helping me pick out Nick's wedding gift?"

He grinned. "Yup. Just now," he said meeting Liz's sheepish gaze.

"Liz, this is adorable." Rosie met her gaze after opening the gift she'd brought for the birthday girl who was more interested in the paper than the present. She held it up so everyone could see. "It's a wooden puzzle that spells out Stephanie's name."

"I'm glad you like it," Liz said.

After a dinner of barbecued steak, baked potatoes and a big Italian antipasto salad, the family had gathered underneath the brick patio for gift opening. Surrounded by a tricycle, an orange and yellow plastic car, and other toys too big to wrap, Rosie and Steve had taken over the task of opening the waiting mound of gifts to speed up the process.

Liz sighed, wishing the lucky little girl would be able to remember this moment and how much this big family loved her. If only every child could know that feeling, it would make growing up as carefree as it should be. She couldn't help wishing that her own formative years had been more untroubled.

Liz sat on a loveseat-sized glider with Joe beside her. Since he'd found her with Alex and Luke, he hadn't left her side. As promised. He also hadn't rubbed it in that she'd been wrong to think the worst of him when Abby had called to remind him of the shopping trip. She felt lower than a snake's belly and didn't think the feeling would slither away until she told him she was sorry.

"It's time for cake," Flo said.

She and Tom went into the house and brought out two—one for the adults and a cupcake with a candle in it for the birthday girl. Steve had put her in the highchair set up outside. When her grandpa set the cupcake on her tray, she tentatively touched a tiny finger to the icing. After tasting it, she went after the remainder with gusto.

Liz was completely charmed as the toddler squished her hands in the confection then rubbed it in her hair—to the accompaniment of groans by her parents.

When she had decimated the cupcake, Rosie said to her husband, "Bath time—again."

Steve nodded and lifted her from the chair and the threesome disappeared inside.

Flo put her empty cake plate down on the table. "You know, I just had our home movies transferred to video. Would you like to see them?'' she said to Liz.

''I'd love to,'' she answered truthfully.

She was curious to see what Joe looked like as a boy. Was he always the family charmer? Or had he acquired the talent at the onset of puberty and his attraction to the opposite sex? Not fair, she reminded herself. She'd been proven wrong about him and was deeply ashamed of herself for automatically assuming the worst—again.

The family filed into the house and Liz was about to fall into line.

Joe put a hand on her arm. ''You don't really want to see movies, do you? That's more of a snooze than phenobarbital.''

''On the contrary, I would thoroughly enjoy watching the 'little Joey' show,'' she said with a grin.

He shook his head and automatically blocked her path. ''That does it. You'll have to get past me to see it.'' Then he threw up his hands and in the dim light she saw his grin. ''Look who I'm talking to. Miss Do-as-I-say-or-I'll-twist-your-ear-off.''

Liz couldn't help laughing at him even though she had mixed feelings about her choice of after-dessert entertainment. It was safer inside, surrounded by his family. Outside was a lovely summer evening with a romantic sky full of stars and a full course crow dinner. After learning that the phone call he'd received had been perfectly innocent, she owed him an apology. Best to get it over with. When Joe tugged her from beneath the patio cover to a spot by the pool, she didn't protest.

The night was warm, with a hint of breeze blowing. Malibu lights illuminated the whole backyard and the pool area. Joe sat on the edge of the pool and stuck his bare feet in the water. He patted the cement beside him and she only hesitated a second before accepting his invitation. She slipped off her sneakers and dipped her feet into the soothing water.

A big sigh of contentment escaped her. She was amazed how comfortable she was with him now that she'd let her guard down. She'd felt his magnetism right from the beginning and had been fighting against it. Now she knew resisting was an exercise in futility. But before she could completely relax, there was something she had to do.

"Joe, I want to apologize to you."

"Okay."

"I'm sorry I questioned you that day. When Abby called, I automatically assumed it was a woman—"

"And you were right."

"You're not going to make this easy, are you?" She let out a long breath. "Okay. I insist you make it as hard on me as you can. I sure didn't go easy on you. It would make me feel better if you just rub my nose in how awful I was to you."

"Would I do that?"

She slid him a sideways glance. "Yeah. And I don't blame you. Believe me, I'll feel a lot better if you make this just as difficult as possible. I deserve it. My only excuse was that every time I saw you, there was a different woman."

"Ah yes. What was it you said? I had a revolving door for a heart." He grinned. "Not that I owe you, but the tall blonde you saw me with really was my secretary. I told you about her, the one who had a baby. Not only did she drop off a gift for Rosie, she was at the hospital because she was pregnant and having tests.''

"Okay." She nodded, resigned to taking what he had to dish out. She owed him that. Even if he'd been less than a gentleman to one of her co-workers. "However, in my own defense, I have to say that I probably wouldn't have jumped to conclusions if it hadn't been for the way you dumped Trish."

He tensed beside her. "Trish Hudson? You mentioned her before, that day at the beach."

She read the look of intensity on his face and had a feeling she wasn't going to like this. "What?"

"That's what I'd like to know. I wouldn't call our parting of the ways a dump."

"She found you with another woman."

"What?" He stood up and jammed his hands on his hips. Even in the dim light she could read anger, betrayal, and self-righteous indignation on his face. If he was acting, it was an academy award caliber performance. What was going on?

She stood up, too. "Trish said she broke it off when she dropped by your condo and found you with another woman. She admitted that you'd never actually agreed to an exclusive relationship, but she was hurt just the same," Liz finished doubtfully.

He shook his head and there was a bitter twist to his mouth. "Interesting interpretation. And a complete fabrication. But why would you believe a guy who doesn't know the meaning of the word longevity or sincerity?"

"Try me."

Surprise flashed into his eyes. Then he nodded. "I took her out a few times. She was getting serious and possessive. I didn't feel the same way. I prefer to be straightforward and told her that. I said I'd like it if we could remain friends. End of story."

Maybe it was the way he said the words, completely without embellishment, but she knew he was telling the truth. "Now I feel like a jerk, times three," she said.

"You believe me?" he asked, obviously surprised.

"Yeah," she said nodding. "I do. Trish the dish has been caught in a couple of lies—calling in sick to go away for a long weekend, having someone else punch her in when she'd taken a longer lunch. Stuff like that." She shook her head. "Even knowing that about her, I was quick to take her word over yours. Joe, I can't even begin to tell you how very sorry I am. Can you forgive me?"

He paced on the pool deck for a few moments, then stopped in front of her and looked down. The scent of his aftershave drifted to her, making her insides quiver. He was so close, she could feel the warmth of his body. God help her, she wanted him to touch her, hold her. Kiss her? Yeah, that too. Especially that, even though it was not the brightest thing to do.

Finally he said, "Yeah. I forgive you."

His words made her relax, even though she didn't understand how he could so easily let her off the hook. "Just like that?" she asked.

"What can I say? I'm a great guy."

"I'm beginning to see that. Anyone else would have seen that from the beginning. Anyone but me."

"Why is that, Liz?"

His tone—warm, welcoming—invited confidences. If nothing else, he deserved an explanation.

She sighed and sat on the chaise lounge next to the pool. He sat on the matching one next to her and their bare knees brushed, sending a jolt of electricity through her. She pushed the sensation aside. After misjudging him so badly, she owed him an explanation.

"I already told you I'm an only child. As far as I know."

"What does that mean?"

"You remind me of my father, Joe."

"With a lead-in like that, I'm not sure I want to hear this." He laughed without humor. "Not to mention that when a guy is sitting under the stars with a girl, he doesn't especially want to hear that he reminds her of her father."

Her heart pounded. Did that mean he wanted to kiss her, too? If that was true, she was even more humbled. After the way she'd treated him, that he could still be nice to her was amazing.

She met his gaze. "What I meant to say was that I was attributing behaviors to you that you didn't deserve based on what my father did."

"And what was that?"

"He was handsome as sin. He was an unfaithful playboy who broke my mother's heart on a painfully regular basis. I don't ever remember a time when he wasn't cheating on her. From the time I was a little girl I would wake up and find her waiting for him to come home. Sometimes he didn't show up at all. When he did, usually he reeked of perfume and didn't bother to hide the lipstick smudges on his shirt."

He reached over and wrapped his big warm hands around her smaller ones. That comforting gesture sent a feeling through her, a sensation that she was safe and protected. It was something she had never felt before. It was a warm, cozy, wonderful feeling that, oddly enough, made her afraid too. It was something she never wanted to count on because she couldn't trust it.

When she tried to pull her hands away, he wouldn't let her. He held on, gently but firmly, and squeezed reassuringly. "I'm sorry, Liz. That must have been hard for you. And it does help me understand."

"There's more."

He shook his head. "You don't have to tell me. I can see that this hurts you a lot."

"Yeah, but I need to clear the air, get it off my chest. I was terrible to you and you didn't deserve it. I'm so ashamed. My behavior was reprehensible. The least I can do is tell all."

He nodded slowly. "Okay."

She cleared her throat. "Mom and Dad stayed together. For my sake. But he was never really there." She thought about the day's birthday festivities and laughed a little bitterly. "Would you believe I was envious of Stephanie tonight? Pretty funny, huh?"

"Why?"

"Because everyone in this family loves her enough to take time out of their busy lives to acknowledge her first birthday. And except for the pictures, she won't even remember." She looked at the pool, the light at the bottom. "It was usually just me and Mom on my momentous occasions."

"Your dad didn't show, not even for birthdays?"

She shook her head, willing the tears she'd never shed not to fall now. "Not graduations or awards ceremonies or prom night. Why would he when the flavor of the month was so much more exciting?"

"Where is he now?" There was an angry edge to his voice.

She'd never heard that particular tone from him before. Was it on her behalf? What would he say if she told him it got to her even more than his charm?

"He died the year I started nursing school. My mother had thought there was life insurance. But he'd borrowed against it until everything was gone. No doubt he had to spend money to impress whatever woman was in his life. Mom and I moved to a smaller apartment. I worked my way through school."

"What happened to your mom?"

"She died about a year after he did. I suspect of a broken heart. She loved him, in spite of the fact that he didn't know the meaning of the word faithful. Unlike your parents."

"Yeah," he said grimly. "Thanks to them, I'm no longer looking for someone."

Chapter Five

"I don't understand that." Liz was sincerely interested in his answer.

Now that he'd shot down her suspicions, she really and truly wanted to believe he was telling the truth. She wanted to trust that he wasn't just fabricating this story to lull her into a false sense of security. But it was awfully hard to swallow. As a boy, he'd grown up in a stable family. As a man, he had everything—looks, enough personality to charm a determined hermit, and financial security. If nothing else, women would come on to him in mind-boggling numbers increasing the probability that he would find someone. Why would a guy turn his back on that? And what did his parents have to do with his decision?

Joe let her hands go and ran his fingers through his hair. The gesture was almost angry. He stood up and his big body blocked out the Malibu lights, putting her in the dark.

"I'm a pretty competitive guy," he said. "It's not

always a good thing. I tend to calculate my chances of success. I hate to lose.''

''Funny, I thought we were talking about romance. I was paying attention. I missed the transition to a marathon.''

''From what I've seen love makes the iron man competition look like an ice cream social.''

''Really?''

He turned and met her gaze. ''I've watched guys I went to high school and college with fall in love, or a reasonable facsimile thereof. The next thing I knew, they'd split for one reason or another and then it's all about hurt and blame and making the person they supposedly loved pay. Alimony, child support, not to mention the emotional cost. A friend of mine is going through hell right now. His ex is using the kids as a weapon. She makes his life miserable, changes the rules, holds him to the letter of their agreement. No flexibility at all. It stinks.''

''That's a shame. Everyone loses. Especially the children. Take it from someone who knows.''

He put his hands on his hips. ''It seems wrong to use the legal system for revenge.''

This was a side to him that surprised her, a depth she hadn't suspected. She'd thought he was all charm and as shallow as a puddle. For some reason she felt the need to poke holes in his cynicism, bolster his boyish enthusiasm.

''Surely there are happy couples out there. What about Rosie and Steve?''

He shrugged. ''That's different. They've known each other since they were kids. I think they've always been in love.''

"I'm not sure why that's different. But, okay." She thought for a minute. "Nick and Abby?"

"Same thing. They have a long history together. Nick gave her her first job and helped her after her folks died in a car accident. She raised her younger sister Sarah and he was there for both of them."

"And suddenly it turned to love?"

"I hear that skeptical note in your voice. I wouldn't describe it like that exactly. I think it was always there from the moment they met and it just took time for them to figure it out."

He met her gaze. "Okay, and then there's my parents who have been together over three decades. They're disgusting the way they still hold hands, make goo-goo eyes, etcetera."

"I think that's sweet."

"Yeah. But given today's divorce statistics, who can match that?"

"So you're not going to try?"

"I have tried."

"A lot?" she asked. She attempted a teasing note in the question, but found the subject still rubbed a raw spot inside her. Why? What possible difference could it make to her whether or not he had dated a lot? She had no intention of being next in his line of hopefuls.

He smiled. "I suppose a lot. I've met quite a few women."

"I'd be surprised if you hadn't." A guy as good-looking as him would have to barricade the door of a monastery to keep the hussy hordes at bay.

"You didn't let me finish. I've met and dated a lot in my time, but I don't think love is in the cards for me."

"Because it hasn't happened?" Say yes, she thought, not willing to analyze why she cared whether or not he'd been in love.

"There's been no one special for the long haul. And because of the example my parents set and all the pain and misery I've seen—failure is not an option."

"So you're giving up?"

"I wouldn't put it like that. Stopped looking is more the way I see it. I choose not to try. There's a difference. Somehow it seems nobler to take yourself out of the game than to play handicapped and blow it completely."

"I suppose." She shivered.

"Are you cold?"

"It's getting chilly," she admitted.

"I can do something about that." He held out his hand.

Her heart beat double-time as she put her cold hand in his warm, strong one and let him pull her to her feet. "What did you have in mind?" she asked, looking up—way up—at him.

Most guys would go straight to something physical to warm her up. What would he do?

He linked his fingers with hers and led the way past the pool and toward the brightly lit house. "I need to get you inside before Regional Medical Center's star baby nurse gets sick."

Liz felt a momentary prick of disappointment not to mention frustration. Nine guys out of ten would have opted for combined body heat and probably a kiss leading to whatever he could get away with. Why did she find it so annoying that he'd picked this opportunity to prove yet again that he was a ten?

* * *

Joe was taking a break from his volunteer shift while the babies were with the mothers. On his way to the cafeteria for a soda, he passed classroom 2 and realized that this was the night Liz held her new mothers' support group. He poked his head in the back door, just to see what was going on, he told himself. Not because it had been two days since they'd been together at his folks. And not because he'd been keeping his eyes open for her ever since he'd arrived right after work and had been disappointed at not seeing her cute, curvy, cheery little person.

She was in the front of the room listening intently to one of the moms and didn't notice when he slipped into the room and took a seat in the back. All the better to watch her.

Tonight she wore hospital scrubs—teal-colored cotton pants with an elastic waist and a V-neck top covered with cartoon characters cavorting on a white background. Certainly not a femme fatale ensemble, but eminently practical for her job. Oddly enough, shapeless clothes and all, she looked pretty darn good to him.

He watched her bite her lip as she focused on the woman's words, something about not being interested in what got her into this in the first place. It was the darnedest thing. Why had he not realized what a kissable mouth Liz had until he *hadn't* kissed her?

Ever since she'd told him her history, he hadn't been able to concentrate on much of anything but her. Visions of Liz under the stars kept popping into his mind. He'd thought about kissing her. He'd wanted to. The way she'd looked up at him with her big eyes and all, he'd sensed that she wanted him to kiss her, too.

But he decided it would be best not to live up to her low expectations. Unfortunately, his body didn't get the logic. The more he watched her now, the worse it got. Maybe absence was the antidote. He decided it was time to leave. When he stood, the chair backed up a notch and the resulting squeak seemed loud as a gunshot. All heads in the room turned. He froze, like a deer caught in headlights.

"Hey, Joe." Barbara held up a hand in a wave. "Got any more words of wisdom?"

"Excuse me?" he said.

Andie, the mother with breast-feeding questions, chimed in. "You were amazing the last time you dropped by group. I bet you can give us some great advice about this."

He'd been concentrating on Liz's mouth and hadn't a clue what they were talking about. But it was safe to say whatever it was probably wasn't for a man's ears. "I didn't mean to intrude. Actually, I just came in to sit for a minute until visiting hours are over and the babies go back to the nursery."

There was a twinkle in Liz's eyes as she said, "For our new moms, let me introduce you. This is Joe Marchetti, our most recent addition to the cuddlers program."

"Hi," he said with a quick wave.

He recognized Andie and remembered her baby's name was Val. And Barbara was there with Tommy. There were a couple more mothers he recognized and several who looked what he could only describe as "first-couple-weeks-of-infancy haggard."

"No doubt you heard, but let me sum up for you,"

Liz said in a tone that told him she knew he didn't have a clue. "We were discussing what I like to call post-partum lackluster libido syndrome. I've tried to come up with some suggestions to combat this phenomenon in new mothers. They love their husbands. They're anxious to show their love. But they aren't quite *there* yet, if you get my drift."

He groaned inwardly. Here we go with the double-speak again, he thought. The wild thing, you know, the horizontal boogie, and so on. He looked at his watch. "It's almost that time. I wouldn't want to shirk my volunteer responsibilities. My boss is a tough cookie—"

"Not so fast, Joe." Barbara bounced her sleeping infant. "We're talking about the wild thing here. Remember that?"

Did he ever. Since that night under the stars with Liz, it was all he could think about. That and how good she smelled. How soft her skin was when he'd held her small hands. How delicate and feminine those hands were and how it made him want to protect her. And that led him to more wanting—like the touch, texture and taste of her lips—*if* he'd taken a chance and kissed her.

"What about it?" he asked, hoping they hadn't noticed that his voice sounded hoarse.

"It's what brought me this beautiful baby boy. I feel so blessed. And I feel bad for my husband. I love him. But I'm afraid that I'll never want to be with him again. You're a guy—"

"Brilliant, Barb," Andie said with a chuckle. "What was your first clue?"

"The beard and muscles were a dead giveaway," said a woman whose name he didn't know.

"Okay, Christina," Liz said laughing. "We don't want to embarrass our guest speaker."

"Are we making you uncomfortable, Joe?" Barbara asked.

"No," he said and found it was true. Only one woman in the room made him uncomfortable. She was wearing shapeless scrubs and had a kissable mouth.

For half a second he thought he might have said that out loud. When they didn't look at their fearless leader and snicker, he figured there was no need to duck and run.

But he realized he truly wasn't embarrassed about the subject matter. This was an earthy group of women who were at ease with talking about this perfectly natural subject.

"Do you have any advice?" Liz asked, tapping her top lip with her finger.

There it was again. His pesky inclination to trace that exact spot with his tongue. "Well," he said, then swallowed hard. "I would start with kissing."

"How's that?" Liz asked. He wondered if it was wishful thinking on his part or if she actually sounded a little breathless.

"Take baby steps," he continued. A general giggle erupted. He grinned at the group as he moved to the front of the room. "You and your mate have been through the most intimate experience a couple can share. But life is a series of trade-offs. Having a baby brings you closer."

"I hear a but," Christina said.

He nodded. "The demands of an infant can drive a wedge between you if you're not careful. Make time for each other. Start with kissing—no expectations for either of you. Then just holding. Again no expectations. Before you know it, the wild thing will just happen. Like anything fragile, libido needs raw material to help it grow. I suspect if you start slowly, you'll find yourself really getting into it.''

''You make it sound easy,'' Barbara said, sighing loudly.

''It is. Finding a window of opportunity and wedging it open is the tough part.'' They all laughed.

''How do you know so much about this?'' Christina asked. ''Are you married?''

He shook his head. ''But I have a sister who's gone through what you are now. As a matter of fact she and her husband must have had opportunity and motive because she's expecting her second child in a few weeks.''

Christina laughed ruefully. ''That's going to make it darn near impossible to pry open that window of opportunity again.''

''That's what uncles are for.''

''And I think we'll stop there. Our time is up for tonight,'' Liz said, looking at her watch. ''Good night, ladies. See you next time. Thanks, Joe. Your advice was basic but sound. I think we forget how important touching and holding are.''

A murmur of thanks came from the women gathering up babies, bags and belongings before they filed out.

''That's high praise from a tough taskmaster like you.'' He looked down at her.

''I mean every word.'' She smiled and headed for the doorway. ''See you around. Good night.''

'' 'Night,'' he said to her back.

He liked talking to her and had hoped she'd stick

around. But why should he care when she didn't? She'd seen the downside of commitment and he'd stopped believing.

Maybe it was for the best. Definitely for the best.

Liz had put in an hour catching up on paperwork and was just on her way out the door when she heard her name paged. The nearest phone was at the volunteer sign-in desk. Unfortunately, so was Joe Marchetti. She was having a tough time fighting off thoughts of him that kept creeping into her head. Double whammy. An intimate conversation under the stars where his deep voice had mesmerized her. And then he *hadn't* kissed her. That was a combination difficult for a cynic like her to resist. Difficult because it had become her habit to believe the worst first and ask questions later. The question was why hadn't he made a move on her?

Was it because his family was only a few feet away inside the house? He didn't find her attractive? Or was he telling the truth and just wasn't interested in a serious relationship?

He finished signing out, then looked up. When he spotted her, a wide grin turned up the corners of his mouth. "Hi," he said. "Didn't they just page you?"

"Yes," she answered, lifting the receiver on the desk beside him. Her hand shook and she turned her back so he wouldn't see. "Liz Anderson," she said into the phone.

"This is Ernie from the Office Supplies Warehouse."

"Please tell me my computer desk is all together in one large, attractive and ever so functional piece," she pleaded.

"Wish I could. But because of the sale and employees out with the flu we're backlogged two to three weeks."

"Three weeks?" she cried. "My computer is scattered all over a card table and begging for a home."

"Sorry. We'd be happy to refund your money if you'd like to look somewhere else."

"No. I love that desk. It's perfect for my decor at home. And the price is too good." She sighed. "I've waited this long, I suppose another three weeks isn't so bad." She felt a tap on her shoulder and turned around.

"May I be of assistance?" Joe waited expectantly.

"Hold on, Ernie," she said into the phone. Liz stared at Joe. "What?" she asked.

"I couldn't help overhearing. You bought a desk on sale. You're disappointed because the assembly is delayed for three weeks. I'm volunteering to put it together."

"I couldn't ask you to do that."

He frowned. "You don't trust me?"

"I didn't say that."

"I listen between the lines," he said.

"It's a major imposition," she countered.

"How do you know? I'm pretty handy."

She couldn't help glancing at his wide, strong forearms, revealed because he'd rolled up his shirt sleeves. Beneath his white shirt, she could almost see the muscles in his upper arms, the contours of his broad chest and the harnessed strength there. If he'd been wearing jeans and a T-shirt, she could believe he was a handyman. Good with his hands. And she wasn't thinking about assembling desks, she thought with a shiver.

"You're volunteering to put my desk together?" she asked.

"Yes."

"Sight unseen?"

"I've seen you." His eyes twinkled.

"I was talking about the desk and you know it. You have no idea what it looks like or what kind of challenge it might be to put together. It could be the super deluxe model with two hutches and a top-of-the-line return."

"Risk is my middle name."

She couldn't help laughing. "Are you sure?"

"Absolutely, it's what friends do," he said. "But there's a price."

Ah, she thought. Here it comes. But there was a rebellious part of her that couldn't help getting excited about the possibility of a pass. A part of her that thought experiencing a kiss and then some with Joe Marchetti would be worth the disillusionment later.

"A price? And that would be?"

"You have to call for the pizza."

"Okay." Relieved, she nodded and put the phone back to her ear. "Ernie?"

"First delivery on Saturday morning is eight sharp," Ernie answered. "Meat lovers pizza with the works and a beer should cover his tab."

"Thanks, Ernie," she said laughing. She hung up the phone and turned to Joe.

"Who's Ernie?" he asked frowning.

"What time can you be there on Saturday?" she asked, ignoring his question.

"How well do you know this guy?"

"The desk parts and instructions will be at my

place at eight. If you need your beauty sleep, noon is fine with me.''

"Seven-fifty a.m. is good. I'll bring bagels.''

"I thought food was my responsibility.''

"Your responsibility is to take deliveries—desks and pizzas only. I'll be there in time to back you up. You can't trust guys named Ernie.'' That said, he turned on his heel and exited through the lobby doors that automatically whispered open.

"But,'' she said to herself, "can you trust guys named Joe?''

Chapter Six

Joe closed Liz's front door behind the delivery man and went back to the kitchen where she was making coffee. He needed it this morning and hoped it was ready now. He'd had a problem with insomnia all his life. But since meeting Liz, it seemed to have intensified. Now when he could finally fall asleep, dreams of her disturbed him.

Getting to her place early enough for the desk arrival hadn't been a problem. He'd been awake since around 4:00 a.m. He held back a yawn as he leaned against the center island work area and watched her gather mugs, milk and sugar.

"Late night?" she asked.

"Early morning," he said. He didn't want to share the fact that he'd been awake before God and thoughts of her kept him from going back to sleep.

"Would you like to tell me her name?" she asked, glancing at him over her shoulder. Then she turned back to pour two cups of coffee.

"There is no she," he lied. Her name is Liz, he thought. "So that was Ernie," he said, deflecting her. He took the cup she held out.

Joe hadn't liked watching her talk and joke with another guy. And it didn't make him dance for joy that she was wearing a buttercup yellow T-shirt tucked into khaki shorts that hugged her hips and revealed her shapely legs to that guy. Not to mention her bare feet. He couldn't say why, but her bare flesh, even in limited quantities, made everything seem so much more intimate. Subtly sexy. And it annoyed him that she wasn't even wearing slippers when the delivery man arrived with her desk.

"Do you need cream and sugar?" Liz asked. When he shook his head, she put artificial sweetener and a little milk in her cup. "In answer to your question, yes, that was Ernie."

She'd seemed awfully friendly with him on the phone. Did she like the guy? Did she want to see him again, Joe wondered. And where had that thought come from? He shook his head. Since when had he developed a jealous streak? First his brothers and now this. It was stupid. Since when was he prone to jumping to conclusions? That was Liz's specialty.

Although since the party at his folks, he'd cured her of that particular ailment. But her question about the name of the woman who'd gotten him up early made him wonder. Was she even the slightest bit jealous? What would she say if he told her she was the one who had cost him sleep? And he'd been unable to control his strong reaction to seeing another man in her place.

"Okay then." Feeling a little silly about his out-of-proportion reaction, Joe decided to change the subject. "This is a nice place you've got here."

The remark smacked of "nice weather we're having" or "how about those Lakers," but it was the best he could do. Besides, it was the truth. She did have a nice place.

He'd been to her Encino home in the San Fernando Valley once before, when he'd picked her up for Stephanie's birthday party. But then she hadn't invited him in. She'd greeted him at the door with purse in hand and they'd left.

"I like it," she said, looking around her kitchen. "It's only a year old, but I moved in when it was brand new."

"Wasn't that a lot of work? Window coverings? Yards?"

"I learned to be handy. Blinds aren't that hard to install. And new is what I wanted. No bad history. A clean slate. Only good memories."

Unlike the way she grew up. He wished he could erase all the bad stuff from her slate. All that baggage got pretty heavy to carry around. And he found he very much wanted to lighten her load. But he didn't think that was possible. At least he could show her she had nothing to fear from him. There wasn't anything he wanted from her. At least nothing more than friendship.

"Well, you've sure done a lot with the place in a year," he said.

They were standing on a wood floor. Shiny cream-colored tiles covered the ample counter space. The walls were painted tan with white doors and moldings. White mini-blinds hid all the windows. At the far end of the family room, there was a used-brick fireplace. In a semicircle before it sat a green-and-maroon plaid sofa, loveseat, and two wingback chairs in a coordinating shade. The room was well-decorated, but homey too. At least it felt that way to him.

After looking around, Joe met her gaze. "How big is the house?"

"About fifteen-hundred square feet. One bedroom and a den. Kitchen, family room combination and formal dining room. It's small, but my budget and I like that. It's perfect for me."

Perfectly calculated to keep her personal space from admitting anyone else, he noted. But she was a lady who knew what she wanted and where she was going. He liked that. In fact he liked everything about her.

"Taking a wild guess, I bet that desk is going in the den." He blew on his coffee, then took a sip.

Faking amazement, she shook her head. "You are just full of surprises, Joe. You're not just all brawn and no brains. There's some intelligence tucked away behind that pretty face."

"Yeah, yeah. I'm a sure thing, lady. You don't have to use flattery to get the job done."

"And speaking of the job, those boxes are waiting in the den."

"Plural? As in more than one?" he said skeptically. "It really is a big desk."

She led the way down the short hall to the room across from her bedroom. "Don't say I didn't warn you."

He watched the seductive sway of her hips and ruefully acknowledged that he needed a warning. But not about the ups and downs of desk assembly. She had a trim back and narrow waist. Her graceful, sexy movements were guaranteed to make a man sit up and take notice. She hadn't warned him about that. Not to mention the lush curves of her thighs that tapered to shapely calves and ankles. She was *so* not his type. His taste ran to tall, statuesque redheads. Liz was compact, curvy and cute. But man, oh, man. She packed a powerful punch in that petite body. Her rounded derriere was just the right shape and looked soft—the kind of soft that invited a man's touch.

Whoa, Joe. Suddenly he was glad that Liz kept her distance, because thoughts like that could take him to a place he didn't want to go—no way, no how. If he went there, it was a surefire way to send her running for cover. He found he wanted very much to have her around. The best way to do that was hands at his sides, nose to the grindstone.

But he couldn't help peeking into her bedroom. The quick look gave him an impression of utter femininity—queen-sized four-poster bed, floral spread, lots of pillows in shades of green, maroon and pink. And lace. That den of delicacy begged for a man's presence, if nothing else to help Liz tangle the sheets beneath that tempting coverlet. He pushed that thought away, wondering if it was a mistake for him to have volunteered to help her with anything. Sharing her space gave him all kinds of ideas.

She walked into the den and surveyed the two long, flat, rectangular cardboard boxes. "Here it is. Hard to believe the large, three-dimensional piece of furniture I fell in love with fits in those tiny boxes," she said ruefully.

"Never fear," he said. "Marchetti is here."

"I'd feel better about that statement if you were a

construction worker instead of a people person." She rested her hands on the hips he'd so recently admired. "I don't suppose the Human Resources Director has much experience in the field of building furniture."

"Resources is the key word," he said. "I'm a resourceful guy. No job too big, too small, too challenging."

"I'll go get my tool box."

He lifted one eyebrow. "Liz Anderson, tool chick?"

She grinned. "Joe Marchetti, carpenter dude?"

He grinned back. "Touché."

Liz slid her chair away from her kitchen table, stood up, then picked up Joe's empty dinner plate as well as her own. A very late dinner, she thought. But well worth it since her desk was assembled and organized. Joe had done a wonderful job, especially since the directions were about as long as *War and Peace* and as complicated as the Russian translation. She had ordered pizza for lunch, but as the hours of frustrating work added up, she knew a meal cooked with her very own hands was definitely what the toolman deserved.

"Let me help you with the dishes," he said standing, too.

"Are you kidding?" she protested. "You've done more today than one simple home-cooked meal can repay. No way do you have to help with cleanup."

"That chicken was great," he said.

"I wasn't fishing for compliments."

"And I wasn't saying it just to flatter you. I sincerely enjoyed your cooking. Just be gracious and say thank you."

"Thank you. I choose to believe you. And from a restaurant-type person like yourself, that was high praise."

"I still want to help you clean up." He put his hands on lean, jean-clad hips as he stared down at her.

She hadn't been prepared for her powerful physical response to his presence. Her breath caught at that ultra-masculine pose, not to mention the snug T-shirt that teased her imagination about what was underneath. Her imagination was just getting warmed up she realized, as her gaze wandered over his worn jeans covering muscular thighs.

All her gazing added up to torment for her nerves. As grateful as she was to have her desk, she was wondering if it had been a mistake to accept his offer of help. She'd meant what she'd told him about her house having no memories. Well, today she'd made a whole pile of them, and every last one starred Joe Marchetti.

"Okay, you can help with the dishes," she said, her voice a husky version of her norm.

He nodded, then took two long strides to the sink where he turned on the water. He lifted a plate and started to rinse, wincing when water splashed on a nasty cut he'd acquired in the line of carpenter duty.

Liz's bedside manner kicked into high gear. "Okay, hero, it's time to dress that battle wound." She reached over to shut off the faucet.

He glanced at his thumb, the slash where his screwdriver had slipped and gouged a long crevice. "It's just a flesh wound. No big deal."

"This is me you're talking to. Never fear, Nancy Nurse is here. No laceration too big, too small or too challenging. Just wait here while I go get a needle and thread from my sewing kit.''

A skeptical look crossed his face just before he ever so casually stuck his hand in his pocket. ''No offense, Nancy, but I'd like a little novocaine with my sutures.''

''You? Just-a-flesh-wound Marchetti?'' She grinned. ''Don't be a wimp. I've got a turkey baster you can bite down on.'' She turned away and started down the hall.

''Liz,'' he called. ''You really don't have to do this.''

''You don't want to have a big, ugly, scar marring that perfect body, do you?'' Take it lightly, she thought, as she rummaged through her medicine cabinet. She carried her supplies back into the kitchen.

Joe inspected the disinfectant, ointment, and bandages she plopped down on the table. A wry expression turned up the corners of his attractive mouth. ''You were pulling my leg,'' he accused.

''Would I do that?''

''Yes. And take great satisfaction in making me squirm,'' he added.

''I'm not kidding now, Joe, this really does need to be cleaned up. Infection can be nasty and painful. An ounce of prevention is worth a pound of cure.'' She took his big hand into her smaller one.

The difference in their hands made her feel delicate and feminine to his bigger, tougher masculinity. That thought started her insides buzzing like a beehive at peak pollinating time. He had nice hands—long, strong fingers. She put the brakes on that train of thought before it could go any farther, like how those hands would feel holding her, touching her. Grabbing the brown plastic bottle of peroxide, she pulled him over to the sink.

"This won't hurt a bit," she said, unable to keep the twinkle from her eyes.

"You told me you're lying when you say that," he protested.

"Don't be a baby. How bad can it hurt? This little scratch hardly slowed you down today."

As she held his hand over the sink, their forearms brushed and bumped. Her breast scraped his arm and she thought he sucked in a quick gulp of air. Although she was disinfecting his wound at the same time so she couldn't be sure stinging pain wasn't what had caused his reaction.

"We need to let that bubble for a bit," she said. She liked holding his hand. She liked being close to him, and enjoyed the scent of his aftershave as it burrowed inside her and started the buzzing all over again. How long could she keep him in this position without him getting suspicious, she wondered.

She reveled in his strength. His company wasn't bad either. He was charming and certainly not hard on the eyes.

"After we clean up the kitchen, want to watch a video?" The words were out of her mouth before she had a chance to think about them. Part of her wanted to call them back. Part of her was afraid he would turn down her offer.

"Sure," he said.

"I just picked up a previously-viewed action thriller at the video store."

He held up his wounded hand. "You haven't seen enough blood today?"

"Or I have an old musical guaranteed to clear the room of testosterone in five seconds flat."

"Let's go with video number one. I'd hate to deprive you of your plasma quotient. Besides, if it's new, you should check it out and make sure there's nothing wrong with it."

"Right," she said, pretending to go along with his thought process. She poured a little more peroxide on his thumb. Couldn't be too careful.

"I have something I'd like to ask you," he said.

Her body tensed. Habit sent her to the place where she believed badly of what he was about to say. She shook off the feeling. Anger bubbled up inside her as strongly as the peroxide on Joe's thumb. Her father and his chronic unfaithfulness had made her distrustful. She hated that he'd robbed her of the ability to meet a man without automatically assuming he was a deceptive jerk who would make a fool out of her.

"Okay. Ask away," she said with a bright smile.

"You know my brother Nick is getting married in four weeks."

She nodded. "A June wedding. What about it?"

"Would you like to go with me?"

She halted in the act of dabbing at the moisture on his hand. "Me?"

"Yeah. We're friends and you would be doing me a big favor."

"How's that?" she asked.

"Number one, it would get the meddling Marchettis off my back. Ma never misses an opportunity to play cupid. She keeps asking me if I'm bringing anyone and uses the excuse that she needs a head count for the caterer. Number two, there's the problem of someone to ride shotgun for me."

"Excuse me?" she asked.

"Every wedding I've ever been to has an unattached female looking to go home with an unattached guy in the wedding party."

"You're one of the groomsmen?"

He nodded. "I'm the best man. And before you have a field day with that, it's the traditional title, not my own comment on my character."

She bit back a grin as she dabbed cream on his cut. "I wasn't going to say a word."

"Uh-huh."

"Except that being the best man would make you the best target." Even if he wasn't good-looking enough to give whiplash to a parade of nuns.

He ignored her comment and continued. "Anyway, if you come along as my guest, I won't have to worry about predatory females and I'll be able to enjoy my brother's wedding day."

"Your cover?"

He thought for a moment and said, "You could say that. So how about it? Will you go with me?"

"Yes. For two reasons. Number one, I really like your family and I would very much enjoy seeing them again. Number two, you held back. You didn't say I owe you for this whole desk thing and you easily could have. But if I can repay the favor by riding shotgun to protect your virtue, then I would be happy to."

"Good," he said.

After putting ointment on his hand, Liz finished up with a very large Band-Aid. She gave Joe her stern nurse look. "I'm about to give you the benefit of my medical experience in layman's terms. Keep this boo-boo clean and don't get it wet."

He saluted. "Aye, aye. In that case, do you mind if I make a phone call?"

"Help yourself. Phone's in the office."

He nodded. "While I'm there, I'll make a notation of the wedding date on your calendar."

While he was gone, she refused to give in to suspicions of him calling another woman. He had every right to call anyone he wanted. It could just as easily be a guy he needed to touch base with. One of his brothers. It was none of her business. The jealousy spreading through her like a tidal wave could easily be explained away. Right, she thought disgusted. And maybe she would flap her arms and fly to the moon.

A few minutes later, he returned. "Did I stay gone long enough to get out of work?" he teased.

"Your timing is perfect," she answered, folding the dishrag and settling it on the divider between the two sinks. "Now you get to relax."

She led the way into her family room and inserted the video into the VCR. She grabbed the remote control and sat down on the sofa, too late realizing her mistake of picking her territory first. He took the spot right beside her, so close that their arms and thighs brushed. Did he feel the sparks as warmly as she did? Why couldn't he have picked the other side of the couch, the chair across the room, or a place in another county? But she decided not to say anything to her hurt handyman. After all, he'd injured himself helping her. Not only that, she didn't want him to think she had feelings for him other than friendship. Because she didn't.

He released a sigh that sounded tired. "Any time you want to start the movie," he said.

She pushed a button and watched the trailer appear

on her TV screen. Joe put his arm around her. Is that what friends did? She'd dated guys and had even gotten very close to one. But no guy had ever been her friend. She had no experience at this. But again she decided protest would bring more scrutiny to her feelings than she wanted.

She concentrated on the images flashing across the screen to keep her mind off the man beside her. But the faint fragrance of fabric softener that clung to his T-shirt, the pleasant smell of his skin, the warmth of his body all combined to increase her breathing. Flutters started in her stomach and if she took her own pulse, she knew it would be elevated.

Not again, she thought. This was probably the least romantic setting she could imagine. Certainly not in the same league as the night they'd sat by the pool under the stars. But darn it, she had the same feeling now as she had then. Nary a star in sight and she wished that Joe would kiss her.

She glanced at him, a surreptitious look. What she saw made it safe to inspect him as closely as she wanted. His eyes were closed. His breathing was deep and even. His body slack and relaxed. The man was asleep!

"I didn't mean for him to relax quite this much," she said wryly. She waited for his eyes to open, but he didn't move.

"I guess I'm about as exciting as dirt," she said, resigned to the situation.

He didn't respond.

Hurt in spite of herself, she tried to move away from him, sliding forward on the couch. He mumbled something as he leaned sideways and stretched out, his long legs hanging off the end of the sofa. When

Liz tried to stand, he tightened his hold, circling her waist with his arm. She couldn't break his grip without a struggle and that would wake him. In spite of her pique, he'd worked very hard today and she didn't have the heart to disturb him.

"I guess we really are nothing more than friends," she said with a big sigh.

That thought should have pleased her. Instead sadness burrowed inside her clear down to her soul. And for the life of her she couldn't figure out why.

Chapter Seven

Joe felt movement beside him and tightened his hold on the warm, soft, curvy body snuggling there. Liz, he thought with a smile. The sensation of her next to him was incredibly pleasant, profoundly relaxing and he never wanted to move. He wanted to stay like this forever. He felt himself drifting off again.

But a small noise got his attention and relaxation vanished in a heartbeat. Was that a sniffle?

He opened one eye. His sleep had been so deep, so peaceful it wasn't easy to clear the cobwebs. When had he last rested so completely? He couldn't remember.

He was on his side, Liz's back pressed to his front, with his arm encircling her waist. The end credits of a movie scrolled by on the television. He realized he'd fallen asleep on her couch. Man what a jerk! He couldn't go to sleep in his own top-of-the-line bed. Why her couch? But that wasn't the worst. Was she crying?

He sat up quickly, trying not to feel guilty that he felt more refreshed and rested than he had in a very long time. "Hey." He rubbed a hand across his face. "I hate sad endings," he said, hoping that and not his being out for the count had produced her sniffles.

"Hey, yourself, sleepyhead. Nice try, but I'm calling your bluff. You obviously slept through the entire movie."

"Yeah. I can't believe I went out cold in about a second and a half. I guess the desk construction took more out of me than my pride would admit."

She slid into the corner of the sofa and pulled her knees up to her chest. "Don't worry about it."

Joe didn't miss the hurt in her eyes. He remembered her confession about her father's carousing and recalled her question that morning when he drank his coffee. She thought he was tired because he'd been out with someone else the night before. She'd kept her voice teasing and her veneer perky. But he'd seen that it bothered her. He refused to examine too closely why anything that bothered her bothered him. He only wanted to reassure her.

"Liz?"

"Hmm?"

"I just want you to know I'm not dating anyone else."

She had started to run a hand through her pixie hair and stopped. She went completely still. "Dating? Anyone else?"

He held his right hand up. "Scout's honor. I didn't believe in playing the field when I actually was looking for someone. And it was the truth when I told you I'd given up the search for a lasting relationship. I was tired this morning, but not because I was out with another woman last night.''

"I believe you. And I'm not questioning what you're saying. It's just your choice of words."

"What words?" he asked.

"One actually. A very important one. Dating."

He shook his head. Obviously he'd slept so hard his brain needed a kick start. He hadn't a clue what she was getting at. "You're going to have to be a shade more specific. I'm at a disadvantage here. I slept soundly on your couch making me the world's biggest jerk. And my mind is fuzzy *because* I slept soundly on your couch. What is it about the word dating that you don't understand?"

"I guess I did assume you were dating someone. I just didn't know it was me."

He nodded. "Completely my fault. I guess I forgot something."

He reached over and tried to tug her closer. When she resisted, he put an arm under her legs and his other arm behind her back and gently lifted her onto his lap. Cupping her cloud-soft cheek in his hand, he lowered his mouth to hers. The single, simple touch, intended only for reassurance, unleashed something inside him, something wild he'd been trying to ignore and suppress.

Her soft sigh of pleasure fed the sensation kicking up the tempo of his breathing. Joe traced the outline of her full lips with his tongue, coaxing, encouraging her to open to him. He wasn't disappointed. Her lips parted and he felt her sweet breath on his face, faint and fast. Slowly, cautiously, giving her the opportunity to change her mind, yet praying that she wouldn't, he entered the honeyed recess of her mouth.

Chest to chest with her, he felt her rapid heartbeat, her soft breasts pressed against him. He felt like he'd died and gone to heaven. And he wanted to take her with him. He slid his fingers through her silky hair and cupped the back of her head, making the contact of their mouths more firm. Her palm curved around his neck. Her fingers toyed with his collar, then slipped into his hair, kicking up his heart rate. Restlessly, she moved her hand, tracing his ear with her finger. The sensation sent a bolt of electricity straight through him. His body hummed with the charge. The blood raced through his veins, painfully and insistently arousing him.

He wanted her.

But as much as he wanted her, he needed to go slowly and carefully with her. It had taken a lot to get her to trust him this far. First base could wait until she was ready.

He cupped her slender shoulder in his palm, and nibbled soft kisses across her cheek, down her jaw, and found a sweet spot just below her ear. He pressed his mouth there and smiled when she gasped her pleasured response. There were layers to his little nurse that waited to be peeled away and he could hardly wait to find the free spirit protected there.

He started working his way back to her mouth when he felt her pushing against his shoulders. "What is it?" he asked.

"Stop. Please."

"What is it?" he asked again, more sharply. He kicked himself for jumping the gun. But his attraction to her was powerful. Otherwise he would have given up on her a long time ago. "Did I do something wrong?"

"No. You did everything way too right," she whispered, touching a finger to her mouth. She shook her head and the frightened look in her eyes disturbed him. "That's why we have to pretend this never happened."

"First, I think that might take more imagination and concentration than I've got," he said. His voice was ragged even to his own ears. He sucked in a deep breath, trying to get his body under control. "Second, *why?*"

Kissing her was the best, most satisfying experience he'd had in longer than he cared to calculate. No way did he want to put it out of his mind and make believe it never happened. He wanted to remember every detail. He wanted to keep kissing her and make more details to remember. He wanted to kiss her on a very regular basis.

As if she could read his thoughts, Liz said, "It can't ever happen again."

"Ever is an awfully long time." Irritation swirled inside him at that thought. Never have the pleasure of tasting and teasing her lips again? Never nibble her neck and hold her while she shuddered in response? They were good together first time out of the chute. With regular practice, they could be a whole lot better. But she had some kind of hang-up. "Why not?" he asked again, trying to tamp down his annoyance.

"Because we're not dating."

"What difference does a label make?" he asked. "We're friends, aren't we?"

"Yes. But friends don't date."

He noticed she didn't say friends don't kiss. He suspected she had been rocked by it as much as he had and didn't even want to say the word. "Is that a hard-and-fast rule?"

She nodded. "Ironclad and unbreakable."

"Also unwritten," he added sarcastically.

Ignoring him she went on. "To maintain an uncomplicated, yet satisfying state of friendship, dating is strictly forbidden."

"Define dating," he said.

She slid off his lap and retreated to her corner of the couch again. "Dating is when you spend time with someone to see if they're 'the one.'"

"The one?"

"Don't play dumb, Joe. I already know how smart you are. You are well aware of what I'm trying to say. Dating is what you do when you try someone out to see if you're compatible. See if you like each other. See if you want to spend the rest of your life with that someone."

"You're making this awfully complicated."

"You started it."

"With a kiss?"

She winced at the word, but nodded. "I'm trying to minimize battle damage here."

"Okay. Tell me what the rule is again."

"No k-kissing." She'd stumbled over it, but managed to say the word.

"If we don't kiss, can we date?"

"You're impossible. And you're splitting hairs." She tried to look stern, but her mouth turned up at the corners. "Dating is a state where two people decide if they can ever have a meaningful relationship. Since neither of us want that, dating is out of the question."

He couldn't help wondering if she was really talking about kissing and dating. Was she afraid of what she felt because it was more than she wanted to feel?

He sensed that debating the issue would tank them right then and there. He wasn't ready for that. Retreat was the better part of valor. "Okay. We're officially not dating."

"Good."

"Then let's clarify. You're still going to run interference for me at the wedding?"

"Yes. But it's not a date. It's a favor, and payback for putting my desk together."

"Whatever you want to call it." He stood up. "I'll tell Ma there will be one more at the reception."

"Okay."

"I think it's time for me to go home."

"It is getting late," she agreed.

Later than she could possibly imagine. Too late for him to take back that kiss even if he wanted to. He went to the front door before he looked at her and followed his instincts straight into more hot water. Nurse Nancy had warned him to keep his wound dry, but he'd ignored the warning and kissed her. And did that mean it would get worse? Since his father hadn't raised a quitter, there was a better-than-even chance that he would wind up in more hot water.

She followed him to the front door. "Good night, Joe. And thanks again for my desk."

"'Night, Liz," he said without looking at her. He turned the knob and let himself out.

When he heard the deadbolt click, he wondered what it would take to unlock her defenses. He wasn't sure of anything except that he was grateful she hadn't changed her mind about accompanying him to the wedding.

Whatever label she felt comfortable putting on their weird vibes, Joe didn't care. He just knew that he wanted to continue seeing Liz.

When she arrived at the hospital for her shift on Monday, Liz was still struggling to get Joe Marchetti off her mind. Work was what the doctor ordered. But as she clocked in, the volunteer sign-in book caught her eye, and reminded her of Joe. More specifically, she remembered his soul-shattering kiss. Here at work, and now at home, there were memories of him.

Every time she looked at her sofa, she went hot all over remembering the way his lips had made her tingle from head to toe. When he'd lifted her onto his lap, she'd suspected he was going to kiss her. She could easily have stopped him. She'd told herself not to go there. But when the time came she couldn't do it. The touch, the taste, the temptation were too tantalizing. She'd called a halt when she realized she wanted more. That scared her. Passing the point of no return with Joe spelled disaster with a capital *D*.

She shook her head as she walked through the double doors and into obstetrics. She automatically glanced at the flow board to see how busy the floor was. Her eye caught the first name—Rosemarie Schafer. Joe's sister? She wasn't due for a couple weeks yet.

She hurried to the labor room. Rosie was hospital-gowned with the fetal monitor hooked up. Joe sat in the chair beside her. Liz was about to ask what was going on when Rosie groaned.

"Here comes another one." She gripped her brother's hand as she rolled from her back to her side and faced the wall. "Push on my back."

He stood and did as she asked. "How's that?"

"Harder," she ground out.

"Honey, if I push any harder, you're going right through the wall."

His tone was a mixture of concern and irritation that Liz knew was directed at himself because he couldn't fix his sister's discomfort and make it instantly go away.

Not wanting to disturb them, Liz backed out of the room. She knew Rosie was on Sam's rotation and therefore in good hands. A million questions went through her mind starting with—where was Steve Schafer? Why wasn't he with his wife while she was in labor? What was Joe doing there? But now wasn't the time.

Several hours later, Liz popped into Rosie's room and found her nursing her brand new son. The second-time mother looked up and smiled, tired but radiant. "Hi. I wondered if you were on duty."

"Hi, yourself." She grinned. "I saw you were here when I started my shift. I peeked in, but you were a little busy. Joe was here and you were in very capable hands with Sam so I decided not to interfere."

"She was wonderful. But I would have been more comfortable with you." She laughed. "Although after a while I don't think I cared. No offense."

"None taken." She walked over to the bed to get a better look at the baby. "He's gonna be a heartbreaker. Looks like his dad."

Rosie studied her son proudly. "I think he does look like his father. But heartbreaker is the last word I would use to describe Steve."

"Speaking of him, where is he? I would have bet

money on the fact that wild horses couldn't keep him from your side at a time like this.''

"He was on a business trip. He didn't want to leave me, but I wasn't due for a few weeks and I insisted he go. I kicked myself from here to the delivery room after my water broke.''

"You were lucky Joe was around.''

"It wasn't luck. Joe knew about the trip. It involved personnel for Marchetti's. When Steve left, Joe moved into my house. Temporary baby watch. When he wasn't guarding me in person, he called on an annoyingly regular basis. He said it would have been Nick's job, but he's too preoccupied with his fiancée and the wedding. So the second son got the nod.''

"And he came through,'' Liz said softly. She remembered the other night when he'd asked to use her phone.

Rosie nodded. "Indeed he did.''

Liz felt a glow around her heart and warned herself. Things that looked too good to be true usually were. She glanced at the flowers taking up every corner of the room. "I thought this place would be crawling with Marchettis.''

Rosie laughed. "I sent them home. Steve, too. He's exhausted. He was up all night trying to get back from his business trip in time for the birth.''

"Did he make it?'' Liz asked. She'd gotten busy and hadn't had a chance to check back.

Rosie nodded. "In the nick of time. This little guy surprised everyone, including his dad and I. But his Uncle Joe was there to pick up the slack.''

"How are you doing?'' Liz asked.

"Absolutely wonderful. Ecstatic doesn't do justice to the feelings I have."

And why not? She had everything, Liz thought. Another beautiful, healthy child, a handsome, doting husband, a large, loving family. Liz was beginning to hate adjectives. All the good ones applied to Rosie Schafer and she, Liz, envied her.

If only she could find a man like that, Liz thought. A memory of Joe, kissing her senseless, popped into her head. That kiss had scared her. It had felt so real, so sincere. If he was acting, she couldn't tell. If only she could believe that he wasn't too good to be true. That the reasons he'd given her for volunteering to cuddle were on the level. Then there was that kiss. It had felt sincere, that he really cared for her. But could she trust that it was an honest, straightforward, bona fide expression of his feelings for her?

Liz sat on the end of the bed. Another pang of envy gripped her when she noticed that the baby's tiny fist rested on his mother's breast. Every day she cared for other women's newborns. And she loved her job. But she couldn't help wondering if she would ever have a baby of her own. Not unless she fell in love, and that seemed unlikely.

"Have you decided on a name?" she asked.

Rosie nodded. "Joseph Steven Schafer."

After his Uncle Joe. Liz smiled. "It has a nice ring to it. Actually he timed his entrance pretty well. You'll be back to fighting shape in time for your brother's wedding."

Rosie nodded. "That occurred to me, too. Abby had asked me to be one of her attendants, but I was concerned about letting her down because of the pregnancy. Now at least I'll get to see my big brother get married. He waited a long time to find the right woman. By the way, I'm glad to hear that you're going to be Joe's date for the festivities.''

Liz nodded. ''I'm coming. But it's not a date.''

''Really?'' Rosie glanced up, one eyebrow raised.

''We're just friends. We're very happy to be friends. We both want to circumvent complications. We're very content with friendship.''

''Really?'' Same word, different inflection. The tone in Rosie's one-word question implied that she didn't buy that explanation for a second.

Liz felt compelled to plead her case. Examples would be good. ''Yes,'' she said. ''In fact Joe fell sound asleep at my place. I think that proves that there's nothing serious between us.''

Rosie sat up straighter in the bed. ''He fell asleep?'' she asked sharply.

''On my couch,'' Liz added, as if that was the piece of information that would solidify her case.

''I don't believe it,'' Rosie said, shaking her head.

''It's true. But it didn't bother me,'' she lied.

''He actually fell asleep on the couch?''

Liz nodded. Now she was concerned that his sister would take him to task for something he hadn't been able to help. Joe was one man who could take care of himself. But for some odd reason, she felt an overwhelming urge to defend his honor. ''He came over to help put my desk together. The store where I bought it was way behind in assembly and I would have had to wait three weeks. Joe volunteered, but it was a much bigger job than he realized.''

''Did you know that Joe's had insomnia for years?'' Rosie met her gaze.

''No.''

"It's true. He's tried everything to get over it. Even participated in a sleep disorders experiment in college. Nothing worked. He didn't say anything about this to you?"

Liz shook her head. Guys always had an angle and if they didn't, they would make one up. Joe had a beaut, but hadn't seen fit to mention it to her. Although it would certainly explain why she'd found him in the newborn nursery before sunup a time or two.

"He never said a word," Liz confirmed. "I guess the good news is that we really are friends. And even dirt is more exciting than I am."

"On the contrary, I think it means he was so comfortable and relaxed with you that he was able to fall asleep easily. It's a sign, Liz."

"A sign of what? That between insomnia and baby watch he had finally sunk to a profound state of exhaustion and there was no stimulus present powerful enough to stave off sleep?"

"No. It's a sign that you two are—" Rosie raised her dark eyebrows suggestively. "You know."

"I don't think so." She stopped short of telling the other woman she was wrong.

"What about the fact that he volunteered to put your desk together?"

"He likes to build things?" Liz asked hopefully.

Rosie shook her head. "He flunked blocks in kindergarten. He hated that stuff when he was a kid."

Liz shrugged. "Then I guess he's one of those people who just likes to volunteer. And insomnia would explain why he showed up for his volunteer shift here in the hospital in the middle of the night."

"What?" The other woman looked confused.

"The cuddler program."

Rosie laughed. "Joe's been known to cuddle, but I wasn't aware that there was an organized program for it."

For the first time, Liz had a bad feeling. "He never told you about his volunteer work?"

"Nope. And no one in the family has said anything either. If they knew about it, it's not the kind of info we could ignore."

Liz's mind raced. Why would he not say anything to his family? Especially if he planned to use his involvement with the program to benefit the family business?

She groaned inwardly. Crow was beginning to stick in her throat where Joe was concerned. It was difficult to capitalize on something he was keeping a secret from the very family the business was named after. Although, why he wouldn't say anything about his volunteer work confused her.

Anger at her father welled up in her. She despised the man for making her into a shoot-first-ask-questions-later kind of woman. Even worse, a nice guy like Joe had paid the price for the suspicious skeptic her own father had created. She'd given Joe the third degree at every turn. His sister had just debunked another of her doubts and Liz felt lower than the lowest single-cell life form. It was a wonder that he hadn't thrown up his hands and refused to bother with her.

"Liz, I think his volunteer work has something to do with you." Rosie's eyes gleamed as she nodded knowingly.

"Me?" While the words warmed her clear to the icy wall she kept around her heart, Liz was afraid, too. Joe was standing in front of that icy wall. Threatening to melt it down with hot looks and hotter kisses. But she was determined not to let him any closer. He was a great guy, but he could still break her heart. She wouldn't be like her mother and let that happen.

"Yeah," Rosie agreed. "You got his attention the last time I had a baby." She looked down at the peacefully sleeping infant in her arms. "Now here I am again and I've discovered that my big brother has a secret life that involves you."

"Secret life?" Liz shook her head. "I wouldn't call us involved."

"Do me a favor. Hurry up and decide what to call you and Joe. Don't make me have another baby to define your relationship."

In spite of her misgivings, Liz couldn't help laughing. Rosie Schafer was easy to like. A quality she shared with her brother Joe, and the rest of the Marchettis for that matter.

"Rosie, trust me. There's nothing to decide or to define. Joe and I will never be anything more than friends."

"Have you ever noticed that when someone protests too much, they always say 'trust me.' No one knows Joe's flaws better than I do, but in spite of them, he's a great guy."

Liz was struggling with that fact. There was no reason that Rosie would lie about his insomnia and her ignorance of his volunteer commitment. That meant one thing.

Joe Marchetti *was* as wonderful as he seemed.

Yikes. That would put a serious crimp in her ability to keep him at arm's length. Unless she could find a

serious defect to sink her teeth into, Liz had to face
the fact that she was up to her ears in trouble.

She had always believed trust was the cornerstone
of a relationship, the raw material necessary to work
up to liking someone. She'd found out the hard way
that she could trust Joe and what she felt was a lot
more than like.

But love? Not now, not ever. No way, no how.
Trust me? she thought. It was out of the question.

Chapter Eight

"Once upon a time, there was a girl named Cinderella."

Joe heard the familiar female voice and peeked through the doorway separating the newborn nursery from the room where employees and volunteers scrubbed and gowned in preparation for handling the infants. He'd just left his sister. She was going home in the morning. Tonight she and her husband were having a quiet dinner in her room.

Liz sat in the rocking chair holding a bundled up baby. A girl. The pink receiving blanket and matching knit hat were a color-coded clue. She wasn't wearing her no-nonsense nurse face. There was an expression that he'd never seen before. A glow of caring, concern, compassion—he wasn't sure how to describe it. He only knew Liz had never worn that particular look in his presence before. He'd thought of her as cute from the moment they'd met. But at this moment, she looked beautiful.

Probably because her guard was down. He knew now that it wasn't personal. Like all kids, she was a product of her environment. Her father, the man she would judge every other man against, had taught her guys couldn't be trusted.

But the vulnerable look on her face now made him want to take her in his arms and never let anyone or anything hurt her ever again. The feeling was so powerful, it rocked him clear through. He'd never felt this way about a woman before.

It was at that moment that he set himself a new mission—to teach her that not all guys deserved to be drop-kicked through the goalposts of life. Some of them were average, everyday joes who put one foot in front of the other in their daily struggle to do the right thing. And he was one of them.

He watched Liz, in profile, glance lovingly down at the infant in her arms. "Cinderella had a hard day, but most days were hard what with a wicked stepmother and two demanding stepsisters whining and complaining. But it got better for Cinderella. Life isn't a fairy tale, but I think you'll like it. Tomorrow will be better."

Joe held his lab coat and stood very still, afraid any movement would alert her to his presence and spoil the spell she was weaving. He stood in the doorway listening as Liz spoke softly and spun the age-old fairy tale right up to the part where the prince slipped the glass slipper on his ladylove's dainty foot and they lived happily ever after.

"So what do you think, little one?" Liz asked, smiling down. Squeaking and squirming from the baby in her arms was the only response. But Liz wasn't a bit put off.

"That's where you're wrong, munchkin. Things worked out great for Cindy. She got her shoe back, she got to call the shots in the kingdom. She got the whole nine yards, the big enchilada, her dream. Plus, she got her fella. It didn't work that way for me. But you," she smiled fondly at the baby. "Your life is a blank slate. You can be anything you want, do anything you want. Go for the gusto."

Joe couldn't help wondering why she was so sure her own dreams couldn't come true. What was standing in her way? In his line of work, he had learned to size people up quickly. He didn't peg her for a quitter. Unless he missed his guess, she would make a class-A mother. He had a feeling she'd make a hell of a wife to a guy smart enough to appreciate her and cherish her. She would be a partner in every way, in the best sense of the word. But she didn't believe she could have it all.

If he hadn't seen so many relationships turn sour, he might be tempted to try and change her mind. But he couldn't get past the ugliness he'd seen after relationship meltdown. He would bet the farm that if you looked in on Cinderella and Prince Charming ten years and a couple of princes and princesses later, things wouldn't be so swell for Mr. and Mrs. Charming. No doubt Mrs. Charming was trying to stick it to him in a financial settlement, and using the kids as a weapon in her quest to take him to the castle cleaners.

Nope, he didn't plan to relinquish his bachelor status. What bothered him, though, was that Liz was the first woman for a very long time who had made him even think "what if." Was it because she wasn't pursuing him the way a lot of women did? Or because she'd made it clear that she couldn't care less? Or that he had to work so hard just to convince her he was really a nice guy? Whatever, she had definitely gotten his attention. No woman in longer than he could remember had made him sit up and take notice the way Liz had.

She glanced over and spotted him in the doorway. A sheepish expression crossed her face. "I didn't know you were there."

"No way did I want to interrupt story hour. Since when are you on cuddler detail?"

"Whenever I can find the time, I like to come in here. It's the only place I know where you can steal a moment of absolute perfection by just holding a small, warm body close."

"I know exactly what you mean," he said softly.

Her big hazel eyes grew just a little bigger and turned a shade greener at his words. Their gazes locked for several powerful moments. Her expression told him she believed he understood those words spoken straight from her heart. It was a flash of crystal clarity, a profound moment when they were on the same wavelength. It was a tiny window of opportunity where he knew if they opened it, there could be something special between them.

Her cheeks turned pink and she looked away, breaking the spell. The window slammed and locked, the curtains closed tight. He wasn't sure if he felt relief or regret. But he figured it was just as well. If she hadn't backed off, he would have. It suddenly occurred to him that one of the things he liked best about her was the fact that she wasn't looking for a relationship any more than he was. He could relax around her, let his guard down. He liked that. A lot.

"What's with the fairy tale?" he asked.

"I don't know. I guess it's silly," she said, sighing. "Maybe just a short retreat from reality. This little girl had a hard day. One minute she was warm, happy, and doing the backstroke inside mom. The next, some big baboon dressed in green from head to toe pushed her out. Then they took her away and started suctioning her. It's a rude entry into the world."

"Seems cruel," he agreed.

"She keeps looking at me with those big, trusting eyes and she'll get this pensive look on her face that seems to say, 'What are you planning to do to me next?'"

"Don't look now Nurse Ratchett, but your gooey marshmallow center is showing."

"A bald-faced lie. My center is hard as stone. There is no weakness, no Achilles' heel. If an ugly rumor to the contrary gets out, I'll deny it," she said. "And speaking of softies, I don't remember seeing your name on the volunteer schedule. What are you doing here?"

That was another thing he liked about her. She could give as good as she got. She was smart and sassy. Kept a man on his toes. Interesting, funny, caring, cute. Enough for a lifetime.

Don't go there, Marchetti, he warned.

He shrugged. "I was here anyway for Rosie and the baby. But visiting hours are over. A certain nurse who shall remain nameless showed me the error of my ways and I'll have you know I vacated my sister's room at the appropriate time without fanfare or force."

She laughed. "Who'd have guessed you were trainable?"

"It's my best quality."

"Do you have any bad qualities?" she blurted out. "Any flaws?"

Joe studied the earnest look on her face and swore she was dead serious. "You of all people should know the answer to that," he said. "Since we met, you've been ticking off my downside at every opportunity."

"Yeah, and getting proven wrong on a regular basis. Why didn't you ever mention that you're an insomniac?"

Uh-oh. Someone in the family had a big mouth. "Where did you hear that vicious rumor?"

"Your sister told me. She said you've been prone to sleeping problems all your life. How come you didn't see fit to mention it?"

"First of all Rosie's always been overly dramatic. It's not that big a deal. Secondly, it's not something a guy usually brings up when he's trying to impress a girl."

The becoming color that suffused her cheeks was the only sign that she'd registered his remark about trying to impress her. And he realized it was true, he had been trying to do just that. He got the feeling that he was nearing the end of his probation with her. That was a good thing, but at the same time it made him uneasy. And he wasn't sure why.

She continued rocking the baby as she looked up at him. "Insomnia explains a lot that you didn't see fit to spell out. Like why you've been known to be here in the middle of the night. And why you fell asleep on my couch."

Actually insomnia didn't explain that last part at all. He couldn't fall asleep on his own state-of-the-art mattress in his very restful condo. So why on her couch? Or was it about her? He couldn't ignore the fact that he liked her—a lot. This nurturing woman who used fairy tales to soothe away the stresses and upsets of a newborn's first hours. This woman could be dangerous to his bachelor status if he let her. But he didn't plan to let her. It was a lucky coincidence that neither of them wanted anything permanent.

"I plead the fifth on falling asleep on your couch. It's just one of those inexplainable phenomenons, like the way an infant no bigger than my forearm can command the attention of twenty adults in a room."

"If you say so."

"I say so," he agreed.

"So tell me more about your flaws." Just then her beeper went off. She stood and put the now sleeping infant back in the isolette. "I'm being paged," she said.

"When do you get off work?" he asked.

She looked at her watch. "About an hour."

He nodded. "Why don't you let me feed you a late supper? I have an in with the best Italian restaurant in town."

"I'm not sure that's—"

He held up a finger. "Do you want a detailed list of my flaws or not?"

She grinned. "You sure know how to sweet-talk a girl."

"It's a management style. Marchetti's my name, Human Resources is my game."

"I'll wait for you by the time clock," she said.

"If you don't take shorthand, a tape recorder works

pretty well to get it all down. And trust me, there will be a lot to get down. I have a very impressive portfolio of flaws. Big ones, little ones, medium-sized ones. I'm a veritable potpourri of flaws.''

She shook her head, but she was laughing. ''I'll remember that.''

''Are you sure you don't mind going to my place?'' Joe asked again. ''I thought you might like to put your feet up. They frown on that sort of thing in restaurants.''

''I don't mind. I'm really looking forward to seeing playboy central with my very own eyes.''

Liz wasn't afraid he would try anything. She'd gotten past that. Besides, she really and truly needed to find some imperfection to help her keep him in perspective. Where better than his bachelor pad? She glanced at him, behind the wheel of his sports car. They'd left hers at the hospital and he'd promised to take her back for it later.

He looked at her quickly, read the teasing in her eyes, and grinned back. ''It's just an ordinary condo. I hope you're not disappointed.''

''Me, too.'' But she was talking about something to keep him at a distance. She sniffed the wonderful odors from the mysterious bag he'd picked up at Marchetti's. ''But if the food tastes as good as it smells, I don't think there's a lot you can do that would disappoint me.''

''Who'd have guessed that the way to mellow you was with the valley's best pasta, a good marinara sauce and some garlic bread?''

''Let's keep that our little secret.''

He made a left turn and drove up into the hills

above the San Fernando Valley. Finally he pulled into the driveway of a condominium complex and parked.

"Here we are," he said, turning off the engine.

"Lead the way. I'm starving."

Joe got out and went around to the passenger door, opened it and held out his hand to help her from the car. Liz placed her fingers in his warm palm and held her breath when a sizzle of awareness zinged through her at the contact. It had been a long time since a man's touch had affected her so strongly. She hoped her willpower was in tip-top shape. Otherwise it was a big mistake to be here with him. But she reminded herself that her assignment was to find the imperfection in this guy. The dealbreaker. Something that would convince her Joe Marchetti was not as wonderful as she feared he actually was.

Liz followed him to his condo and waited while he unlocked the door. He flipped a switch in the entry and the living room blazed with light. Beige carpet stretched in front of her to the dining area with its glass table and floor-to-ceiling windows that showcased a fabulous view of the lights in the valley below. Lots of chrome and leather furniture decorated the room. So he was a glass, chrome and leather kind of guy, she thought. He must have thought her cutesy, country decor was gauche.

She looked at his questioning expression. "So far I have no comment except that your taste in furnishings leans toward the impersonal masculine kind."

"Good. I think," he added with a puzzled look. He had a bag of food in one hand and grabbed her fingers in the other. "Come with me. Penne pasta, salad, garlic bread à la Joe, and a sprinkling of flaws are featured on tonight's menu."

He pulled her into the kitchen, family room combination. Now here was something to sink her teeth into. The stainless steel sink overflowed with dishes sporting everything from dried egg to bowls with left-over cereal that only strategically placed dynamite could remove. Newspapers dotted the countertop, sofa, and table. Sweatpants, jeans and shirts were strewn about the room. A silk tie lay haphazardly over a lampshade.

"Paydirt," she said, nodding with approval. "This is good. Who'd have guessed you're a slob?" she asked brightly.

He set the bag of food on the beige ceramic tile countertop and pulled two plates from the oak cupboard. "I can't help feeling that you just paid me a backhanded compliment."

"How's that?"

"It's not so much that I'm a slob, but that I can hide it so well that no one would know."

She laughed as she riffled through the bag and found the salad, then put it on the table. Looking at a drawer close by, she opened it and found a serving spoon and fork. "That's called compensating for your shortcomings."

"Isn't that what functioning as an adult is all about?"

"Yes."

"Good. Because I found an affordable cleaning service that will put up with me."

"So you have a maid."

"Is that a bad thing?"

She thought for a moment. "No. I could make something of the fact that you don't clean up after yourself. But the fact that you care enough to schedule cleanings for your environment mitigates that defect.''

He poured each of them a glass of red wine and put it on the table. Then he brought over two plates filled with pasta. ''Dinner is served.''

Liz sat down while he opened the refrigerator and pulled out a container. ''What are you doing?''

He glanced at her. ''Gotta have fresh grated Parmesan.''

As he sprinkled some on her food, she inhaled the delicious smells. ''Your culinary accomplishments are definitely *not* a blemish on your record.''

''That's a relief,'' he said.

Finally he sat down at a right angle to her, lifted his glass and said, ''I propose a toast.''

She raised her own glass. ''To what?''

Without a moment's thought or hesitation, he said, ''My new nephew. Peace and long life to Joseph Steven Schafer and family.''

''Cheers,'' she said, clinking his glass before taking a sip.

Interesting that his first thought, his gut instinct was to toast family. He talked a good game about giving up on finding what his folks shared. But no matter what he said, Liz sensed that he wanted that, and what his sister had, and the love his brother Nick had found. What she couldn't figure out was why he was wasting his time with her. Life had taught her that the greatest hurt of all happened because of love. No way did she want to fall. No way would she hand over her heart on a silver platter to any guy. Not even one like Joe Marchetti who approached perfection.

''What are you waiting for?'' he said watching her carefully. ''Dig in.''

"It certainly looks wonderful."

They ate in silence for a few moments. Liz looked at him. "Seriously, Joe, we've been joking about your flaws. But everyone has them. If you could change anything about yourself, what would it be?"

"I'm too stubborn."

"You see that as a bad quality?"

"It can be. Along with a temper obstinance can impair your ability to know when to stay and fight and when to throw in the towel."

"You don't think of it as stick-to-it-ivness?"

"No. I think of it as a character infirmity." He took a bite of salad and chewed thoughtfully for a moment. "What about you? What are your weakest and strongest character traits?"

"Skepticism," she said without hesitation. Then added, "Skepticism."

"Do you want to explain that?"

"I take pride in being cynical. No one is going to get the best of me. Not if I have anything to say about it. At the same time, I miss the innocence of lack of suspicion. But I'm also eminently practical. Life's events shape us into what we are."

"I wish there was a way to undo what your father did. Unfortunately, he left you with an unrealistic outlook of the world in general, and guys in particular."

"What do you mean?"

"Not all men are calculating, unfaithful slime who wouldn't know the meaning of a promise if it bit them in the butt."

Liz's gaze was drawn to him, his sharp tone. He looked angry. "I'm not sure what you're so riled about. I look at it like that song a few years back, 'A

Boy Named Sue'—sometimes you have to be hurt to build up calluses that will get you through life."

"I disagree. Children should be protected from the ugly side of life. Then you introduce them slowly on a need-to-know basis."

"Well I needed to know," she said, wiping the corners of her mouth with a napkin.

"What does that mean?"

"It wasn't only my father. I was engaged once upon a time. I thought I had it all figured out. He was an ordinary-looking guy, in pharmaceutical sales. I met him at the hospital. I thought we wanted the same things and the fact that he was Mr. Every-Guy-in-America would work in my favor on the faithfulness scale. It didn't."

"What happened?" Joe put down his fork and looked at her. There was an intense, angry expression on his face.

Liz felt her heart rate pick up when she realized his anger was for her. Wow. She couldn't ever remember a time when a man championed her, stood in her corner, defended her. This could in no way be construed as a flaw. It could however be a landmine in the field of friendship.

"I found out he was seeing someone else," she said.

"I'm sorry, Liz."

She shook her head. "That was a couple years ago. But that substantiates my point. I had the calluses to help me through that."

"The problem with calluses is that they don't let some of the softer stuff through."

"You're saying it was my fault he turned to someone else? That I was too tough?"

He shrugged. "I'm saying he was scum. And you're better off without him."

"Very diplomatic, Mr. Human Resources Director."

"Thank you."

"So now you know my darkest secret. Tell me more about you."

He put his fork down and gave her a serious, intense look. "I pout when I don't get my own way, I don't like vegetables. And I like to eat my dessert first."

"Wow, a real tough guy," she said, shaking her head.

"Incorrigible, my mother used to say."

Liz enjoyed joking with him. She enjoyed it too much. She'd hoped to find something that would halt, or at least slow her descent into liking him a lot. Not only wasn't a cease-fire happening, she was beginning to heat up more. And not just that. She suddenly wanted to take his handsome face in her hands and kiss him until she could hardly breathe. She wanted to feel his warm soft lips. She wanted him to fold her in his arms where she could snuggle safe and secure.

This was a gigantic mistake.

Abruptly, she stood up and brought her plate to the sink. She opened the dishwasher. The next minute Joe was there.

"Liz?" He took her plate, then turned her to face him. The concerned expression in his dark eyes made her want to cry.

"What is it?" he asked. "What's wrong?"

Chapter Nine

How could she tell him that kissing was her problem?

Specifically kissing him. She was having a devil of a time resisting the urge to wrap her arms around his waist and neck with him until… Don't go there. Turning back would be impossible if that visual took hold. And all because she'd entered the playboy's lair and found out he was endearingly human.

He would get a gigantic charge out of the fact that she hadn't discovered a big, bad flaw to grab hold of, and thus had to conclude that he was really and truly sincere. And now it was entirely possible that the truth of her deep-down feelings would be found out and bared in a toe-curling, heart-stopping, suck the breath from your lungs kiss. And if the above happened, she might just have to take a chance. On a guy. On a guy named Joe.

No. Not a chance. She'd sworn that no guy would ever hurt her again.

"I'm tired is all," she hedged, meeting his concerned, brown-eyed gaze. That was true. It was the coward's way out to take evasive action, but she was suddenly and completely exhausted. "And then there's my crushing guilt for always thinking the worst of you."

"Crushing guilt?" One of his dark eyebrows raised questioningly as the corners of his wonderful mouth twitched in his effort not to smile.

She nodded enthusiastically. "It's a heavy burden for a girl to carry around. Takes a toll. And I feel I must apologize once and for all. I need to go on record that you're one of the most decent guys I've ever met."

He touched her forehead as if checking for fever. "Who are you and what have you done with Liz Anderson, skeptic, doubter, and perky, all-around unbeliever?" He backed up a step, feigning shock. "I don't know what to say."

"There's a first. I thought you were never at a loss for words. Mr. Glib," she said with a grin.

"Not this time."

"It's true. You are a genuinely swell guy who likes children, goes above and beyond the call of duty for a sister in labor whose husband is out of town, and you're nice to your mom. What's not to like?"

"I'm no plaster saint," he said quickly.

"Heaven forbid." She leaned back against the counter and folded her arms over her chest. "But you're not the black-hearted rogue I kept trying to paint you as either. That's all I wanted to say." She stopped. "No, one more thing while I'm humbling myself. I'm glad to count you among my friends," she added.

He frowned. "Friends?"

She nodded. "Believe me it's an honor. I don't think I've ever had a guy friend before. Too complicated. But you're different, in a good way."

"Thanks," he said. Under his breath she thought she heard him say "I think."

"And now, my friend, I think it's time for me to go home." Before she forgot herself and the boundaries of friendship. Before she stepped close to him and lifted her mouth for that kiss she yearned for—and dreaded. Before she couldn't say no to the voice inside her, urging her to see if his mouth was as soft, warm, exciting and stimulating as she remembered.

She had made a lot of mistakes with Joe. But she realized that she truly did want to have him as a friend. And she'd been dead serious when she'd told him that having guy friends got too complicated. One of those complications was wanting to kiss your amigo. She had to get out of here before she made the mother of all mistakes with him.

"Would you take me back to my car?"

"Sure. What are *friends* for?" he said.

He didn't sound happy and she wasn't sure why.

Weeks later, Joe was still smarting from her embracing the friends thing with such cheerful tenacity. He knew she was still ducking for cover with that label, but wasn't sure how to coax her from behind her fortress. What could be better than an idyllic garden wedding to bring out the romance in a girl?

It was his brother Nick's wedding day. Family and friends had gathered in his parents' backyard. Now Nick fidgeted beside the rose-covered arbor as Joe stood up with him. Next came Steve Schafer. Joe felt outnumbered standing between the pro-marriage branch of the family. After him were the confirmed bachelors Luke and Alex, all decked out in traditional black tuxedos.

Joe looked at his older brother. "There's still time to back out."

Nick shook his head. "No way. I've been waiting too long to see Abby in her white dress. Nothing short of an act of God is going to stop me from making her Mrs. Nick Marchetti."

Before Joe could stop it, envy twisted in his gut. He searched out Liz in the crowd. She'd ended the evening abruptly the last time he'd seen her at his place and he'd half expected her to back out of coming today. He was grateful that she hadn't. It surprised him how much he'd been looking forward to seeing her, spending time with her.

Before he could give it any more thought, the chamber music quartet began to play the traditional wedding march. Abby's attendants, including her sister Sarah and Marchetti family attorney Madison Wainwright, filed past the onlookers and took their places on the other side of the arbor. Joe happened to glance at his brother Luke who was staring at Ms. Wainwright with an expression that should be marked "adults only." Interesting, he thought.

Then he looked past the spectators. On the arm of his father, Nick's blond, blue-eyed bride walked down the aisle formed by the rows of guests. Joe spotted Liz, smiling softly at Abby. In a long, full white gown and extended train she was a stunning bride.

Joe thought Liz looked pretty spectacular herself and was in no way shown up by any female present. He'd never seen her dressed up before and had to admit the calf-length, celery-green sheath with short matching jacket that she wore brought out her big, beautiful hazel eyes. Her pixie hair was a mass of curls and pulled back on one side with a rhinestone clip in a sophisticated, sexy style. Sexy because it made him think about pressing his lips to the side of her face bared to his gaze. What would she say if he did that? he wondered.

But he couldn't. Because he would be a fool to get serious about any woman, he reminded himself. Today the flowers and vows, tomorrow court orders, disclosure, and property settlements.

The minister smiled at Tom Marchetti and the woman who would become his daughter-in-law in a few moments. "Who gives this woman to marry this man?" he asked.

"In the memory of her parents, my wife and I do," Tom answered in a loud, clear voice. He turned to the bride, then lifted her veil enough to kiss her cheek. "You've been like a daughter to Flo and I for a long time, Abby. We're proud that our oldest son was smart enough to make you an official Marchetti. It makes us very happy that in a couple minutes, it will be legal and binding."

Joe cringed inwardly. The terms legal and binding made him break out in a cold sweat. Until he glanced at Liz. Then he broke out in something closely resembling lust.

Tom Marchetti took the bride's hand, and placed it in his eldest son's palm. Nick stared at Abby as if he couldn't look at her hard enough. They had been through a lot to be together and Joe sincerely hoped that they would defy statistics and make it as a couple.

When the bride and groom had taken their places in front of the minister, the man opened the book in his hands. He read an inspirational passage about the sanctity of love, vows and fidelity. That should make Liz happy, Joe thought, wishing he could turn around and flash her a grin. Eventually, the preacher got around to the till-death-do-us-part portion of the program.

"Do you Nicholas Thomas Marchetti take this woman to be your lawfully wedded wife?"

"I do," Nick said.

"And do you Abigail Leigh Ridgeway take this man for your husband?"

"Yes, you bet I do," Abby said, smiling sweetly up at her groom.

"Then by the power vested in me by the state of California, I pronounce you man and wife. What God has joined together, let no man put asunder. You may kiss your bride," the minister added.

Nick lifted Abby's veil and pushed it back, revealing her lovely face. "Hello, Mrs. Marchetti," he whispered.

"Mr. Marchetti," she answered.

Then Nick pressed his lips to his bride's and bent her back over his arm for a lengthy liplock that didn't end until laughter, catcalls and whistles got the couple's attention.

Laughing breathlessly, the bride and groom turned to face their guests. The minister introduced them. "Ladies and gentlemen, may I present to you Mr. and Mrs. Nick Marchetti."

Applause filled the air as the newly married couple walked down the aisle. Joe held his arm out for the maid of honor, Abby's teenage sister, Sarah. They followed his brother and new sister-in-law, exiting between the rows of guests.

Before he could make his way to Liz, the photographer herded the wedding party into the house for an official picture-taking session. One by one, each member of the family took a turn posing with the wedding couple. Somehow Joe wound up last. When it was finally over, he went back outside, anxious to find Liz. Music was playing and guests were dancing on the floor that had been set up in the far corner of the yard by the arbor.

The sun had gone down and the lights surrounding the yard were all lit. It was a romantic, fairy tale atmosphere. Unfortunately, it made finding the woman he'd brought a challenge. Because she was five foot nothing and surrounded by people a lot taller. He finally spotted her with Alex and Luke.

It registered quickly that she was laughing and talking with them. Completely relaxed. He'd barely had a chance to say two words to her. And there she was yukking it up with his siblings—his single male siblings. Alex and Luke were only entertaining her as he'd asked them earlier. Why did it bother him seeing her with them?

Suddenly it sank in. He wasn't annoyed with his brothers. He was ticked that Liz was so relaxed with them even though she'd spent very little time in their company. He'd practically had to do cartwheels and a stand-up comedy act to get her to admit that she'd been wrong about him. And there she was having a great time with his brothers. Was her presence at the wedding because of his family? Were the meddling Marchettis the lure instead of himself?

"Hell of a thing," he muttered. Jealous of his own family.

Flo Marchetti appeared beside him. "He who hesitates, gets left in the dust."

Joe glanced to his right and found his mother watching him quizzically. "What does that mean?" he asked.

"It means that I *wish* you had to watch out for your brother Alex."

"Not Luke?" he said. "I thought women came on to him for his bad boy looks and boyish charm."

Flo shook her head. "Unless I'm wrong, and that so rarely happens in matters of the heart, Luke is well on his way to falling like a ton of bricks. And not for Liz," she clarified.

"I hope you're wrong," Joe said, observing his youngest brother who laughed at something Liz said. "And it doesn't matter who," Joe lied, his gut still twisting at the sight of Liz next to his brother. "I hate to see him fall for anyone."

"So you're still a confirmed bachelor?" Flo commented with a sigh, shaking her head in disgust. "I thought when you brought Liz to Stephanie's party, and now the wedding, that maybe you'd changed your mind."

"No way," he said too vehemently. His mother would never know that he'd begun to think "what if" with Liz. If Flo Marchetti got hold of that info, there would be no peace, no place he could hide. "Down, Ma. Someone had to take up the banner now that Nick bit the dust. I'm second in line. It's my job to avoid marriage like the plague and set the standard for my younger, impressionable siblings."

"I see," she said, in a tone that told him she didn't

see at all and refused to believe a word he uttered. "And that's why you're about to walk over there and do battle with your brothers for your date."

He stared at her. "Now I know where Rosie got her overly developed flair for the dramatic." His mother opened her mouth to protest, and he cut her off. "Who's the girl Luke is well on his way to falling for?" He'd long ago learned to take the maternal heat off by deflecting it to one of his brothers.

His mother gave him a horrified look. "Just never you mind about Luke. I would *almost* like to see Alex give you a run for your money with Liz. I'm worried about him. There's no one special, poor boy. I don't think he's ever gotten over Beth."

"I know," he said, feeling for his brother.

"But there's nothing we can do for him tonight," Flo said. "Why don't you go ask Liz to dance?"

"Good idea, Ma," he answered.

"That's the spirit, dear." His mother patted his cheek.

Joe walked over to the trio. "Hi," he said, slanting his siblings a glance. "Thanks for keeping Liz company. But I'm here to claim a dance with the woman I brought." He stared right at Liz, daring her to decline. She didn't say a word, but he thought she tensed.

"She's all yours, bro," Alex said. "I'm going to see how Abby's sister is doing. Mom wanted me to keep an eye on Sarah."

Luke ran a hand through his hair. "I asked Madison to dance. She turned me down flat. Still says the last thing she needs is to get involved with another Marchetti man." He grinned. "But I think I'll try to change her mind. No guts, no glory."

His two brothers disappeared into the crowd and suddenly Joe and Liz stood alone. "Would you like to dance?" he asked.

"Okay," she said, somewhat distracted as she looked in the direction his brothers had gone. "Why would Madison say that, about another Marchetti man?"

"She used to date Nick before he and Abby got together." He took her hand and led her to the dance floor.

Liz craned her neck looking around at the couples. "Interesting that Abby asked her to be a bridesmaid."

Joe shrugged. "They're good friends, always liked and respected each other. Go figure."

The quartet was playing a waltz. At least that was working in his favor. He put a hand at her slender waist and wrapped her fingers in his, leading her into the slow steps. He felt her tension in the stiffness of her body.

"Have I told you how beautiful you look?" he asked.

She nodded. "When you picked me up you said all the appropriate things."

"Well that's a two-compliment dress. And I like your hair that way."

"Thank you," she said glancing away a little shyly. "Have I told you how handsome you look?"

He shook his head. "But I suspect on the heels of that flattery is a zinger to the effect of you've never seen a guy who couldn't be improved by a tux."

"I can't argue with that," she said smiling. "But I'd be less than honest if I didn't say that you make the suit look good."

He grinned back. "Ah progress. It's a good thing."

"Yes," she agreed, watching the bride and groom dance by. "Nick and Abby look happy," she commented. "They only have eyes for each other."

"Yeah," he said sliding his arm more firmly around her waist.

As they'd been talking, he'd felt her discomfort melt away. Her body relaxed and he pulled her subtly closer. She inched her hand up his arm, across his shoulder, until finally curving it around his neck. Now he was getting somewhere.

He just didn't understand why it took him so long to put her at ease when his brothers were there just by showing up. When she'd told him he was a swell guy, he thought he'd made progress. Was he wrong?

Liz sat alone at her table for the first time since Joe had returned from having his picture taken. It was as if he'd set up a perimeter around her, daring any other guy to get past him. Part of her was terrified—part of her was thrilled. The attention was flattering and made her heart go pitter-pat.

If he only knew no other guy was a threat. He was the only one with the power to get to her. She was glad he was busy for a few moments elsewhere. He was so overwhelmingly masculine. So powerfully appealing. So endearingly sweet and funny. She needed a couple moments alone. It gave her a chance to catch her breath. Put her defenses in place for the next assault. In spite of her fears, she couldn't regret her decision to accompany him tonight. She was having a wonderful time. Thanks to his presence.

She suddenly realized she'd had just as good a time putting together her desk, making dinner and watching a movie. Because it was all about spending time with Joe.

Flo Marchetti sat in the chair beside her. "Hi, Liz."

"Mrs. Marchetti—"

"Flo. Please. May I sit down?"

"Of course," she said. "How are you holding up?" she asked.

For a woman in her fifties, Flo Marchetti looked good, and very attractive. Her short silver hair curled around her practically unlined face in a soft, becoming style. No helmet hair for her. Her mother-of-the-groom dress was long and peach-colored with a matching hip-length jacket that flattered her tall figure.

"I'm just fine, dear. Thanks for asking."

"You're welcome. It's a beautiful wedding. Nick and Abby looked so happy when they left for their honeymoon. And you don't look so bad yourself. I love your dress. That satin is so elegant. And the color looks wonderful on you."

"Thank you." Flo laughed. "The kids did look happy when they left, didn't they? I hope the local birds don't get sick from gorging on all that birdseed we threw at the bride and groom. Being environmentally correct does have its downside."

Liz grinned. "You might want to leave the tarp up for a while."

Flo laughed, then met her gaze. "Are you having a good time, dear?"

"Oh, yes," she answered fervently. "Absolutely wonderful. Everything is perfect."

Flo looked serious. "Including Joe?" When Liz met her gaze she quickly said, "I refuse to beat around the bush. I say what's on my mind. And at the moment, that would be information. What's up with you and my son? One minute I think it's serious, and the next either you or Joe is looking completely terrified. Do you have something against him?''

Liz sensed no hostility in the woman, just a genuine desire to understand and help. She smiled sadly. ''No. Nothing. What's not to like about Mr. Wonderful?''

Flo laughed. ''Is that what you call him?''

''Not to his face,'' she admitted.

''Good. He would be insufferable.''

''I recently did an unofficial catalogue of his flaws,'' Liz offered.

''Why?'' Flo asked.

''Because I don't want to care about him.''

''Why?'' Flo asked again, a puzzled frown puckering her forehead.

Liz sighed. ''I don't know how much he's told you about me—''

''Not a word,'' the older woman assured her.

''Well my family put the dys in dysfunctional— before the term became politically correct.''

''You don't have to tell me this,'' Flo said quickly. ''I'm not trying to pry.''

''Yes, you are. And I mean that in a good way. You obviously care deeply for your children and you're trying to protect Joe. I'd like to talk about this, if you don't mind.'' At the other woman's nod, Liz continued. ''My father was a good-looking, charming womanizer. He didn't know the meaning of the word faithful.''

''And your mother stayed with him?''

''Yes. How did you guess?''

"If she'd left, you probably wouldn't be carrying around so much pain."

"She loved him," Liz said with a shrug.

"Then I hope her payback was equal to the energy she put into the relationship."

"I don't know. I'll never know. She passed away."

"I'm sorry."

"But what do you mean about payback?" Liz asked.

"The only reason to stay with someone is if you're happier with them than you are without them. If your mother received enough in return for her loyalty, then I'd say the situation worked for her. If not—" she shrugged.

"How can you get enough back under those circumstances?" Liz asked, trying to tamp down the bitter memories of her mother's tear-stained face.

Flo shook her head sympathetically. "Only the couple in a relationship can judge that. Although ideally two people who stay together should be in love. Otherwise it's not good for anyone, especially impressionable children."

"Divorce is painful too," Liz pointed out.

Flo nodded. "But at least separation gives you time to regroup. The hurtful situation isn't allowed to continue, letting the wounds fester without time to heal."

Liz thought about her words. She could see the wisdom of removing oneself from pain. "How did you get to be so smart? Especially about this stuff? Joe says you and Mr. Marchetti have been happily married for over thirty-five years."

A troubled look crossed the other woman's face. "Most of the years were happy. But we had our ups and downs. We separated for a while."

"Really?" Joe had never mentioned that.

Flo nodded. "It was my fault. Not my husband's. To the best of my knowledge, he has never been with another woman during our marriage. And *he's* a good-looking charmer," she said pointedly. "Joe is his spitting image."

"I've noticed the strong physical resemblance." She wondered if his mother was trying to tell her that Joe would be a faithful husband, like his father.

Liz was tempted to tell the woman not to waste her time persuading her that Joe was a great guy. She was already semihooked. But she decided to keep the info to herself. Right now she was dealing with the stunning news that Joe's parents had had marital problems. Was Joe in the dark about this?

"Tom and I worked things out because we found that we truly love each other. We always have and always will. We are much happier together than apart. Two people with enough motivation can keep a marriage together."

"Do you really believe that?"

"I lived that." Flo reached out and squeezed her hand. "Don't turn your back on something that could be wonderful," she added.

Liz nodded. "I never thought about it like that."

She noticed Joe approaching, a glass of punch in each hand. Her stomach fluttered. And she felt somehow lighter in spirit, as if the heavy burden she'd lugged around all her life had finally slipped away. Her heart swelled with an emotion that was too fragile and new to name. The best news of all?

She wasn't afraid anymore.

Chapter Ten

"Well, look who's here." Liz opened her front door wide.

"Sorry to drop in without calling," Joe said.

She smiled brightly. Was she glad to see him? Sure looked that way. It scared him how badly he'd needed to see her. He was bummed. He wanted to be with her. The warning signals went off in his head, but he ignored them.

"Actually, I was going to call you," she said.

"About something specific, or because I'm a swell guy?"

"You're not going to let me forget I said that, are you?"

"Maybe. When I get equal time for the drubbing you gave me initially. So why were you going to call me?"

"There's a reception for the hospital volunteers Friday night. A small soiree to say thanks. The Board of Directors decided to continue the cuddler program. I thought you might like to be there.''

"Are you planning to be in attendance?"

She nodded. "The staff is bringing the goodies. We're doing the thanking.''

"Then I wouldn't miss it." Or a chance to see her, he added silently.

It had been a couple days since Nick's wedding. He'd been able to think of little else but Liz. It had been a real downer of a day and somehow he'd just wound up on her doorstep. Instinctively he knew that she was good medicine for what ailed him.

"Come on in," she said. "I'm making a salad for dinner. If I add a steak would you care to join me?"

"I'd like that," he said smoothly, trying not to grin from ear to ear.

He hadn't realized he'd been hoping for an invitation until she asked him to stay. They'd had a great time at the wedding. And after his mother had talked with her, Liz had seemed to loosen up even more with him. He liked the way things were between them.

"You look like you've been rode hard and put away wet. Would you like a beer?" she asked.

"I'd be in your debt forever," he answered.

She turned and opened the refrigerator bending down to get what she wanted. His gaze dropped to her backside, encased in soft, smooth sweatpants. Her rounded posterior made his palms ache with the need to touch her, caress her. When she turned around with a longneck in her hand, he forced himself to meet her gaze.

She handed the bottle to him. "Rough day at work? For a Human Resources Director, you look human enough, but I'd have to guess you need a transfusion of resources.''

"Does it show?"

"Yeah," she said sympathetically. "Let's go sit on the couch and you can tell Nurse Liz all your symptoms and I'll write you an appropriate prescription.''

She'd already done that when she opened the door and let him in. He liked that she could read his mood and knew what to do. Maybe too much.

When they sat on the sofa, something made him reach for her hand. She not only didn't pull away, she laced her fingers through his and gave him a soft, tender look. Suddenly he wanted to pull her into his arms and never let her go. He wanted to kiss her and touch her and hold her until all the bad stuff went away. The force of his need made him take two steps back so that he did nothing but stroke the back of her hand with his thumb.

"So what is it?" she asked. "What depleted all your resources?"

"I went to court today. Moral support for a friend of mine who's going through a nasty divorce. They're haggling over the financial settlement." He shrugged. "I was best man at his wedding and now they're splitting up silverware, furniture and kids. Even the family pet.''

"I'm sorry," she said. "What happened to them?"

"Irreconcilable differences," he said bitterly. "A bland, catch-all phrase. A cold, clinical way of saying they fell out of love.''

"Were they ever truly in love?" she asked.

He thought about that for a minute. He went back to that time in college—he and Bill sowing their wild oats. Bill met Jennifer and was in lust with her. They saw each other for a long time until Jenn finally gave him an ultimatum—put up or shut up. She wanted kids, a house, the white picket fence and was ready to walk if she didn't get it. Joe had gotten the feeling that she wasn't the love of Bill's life. His friend just didn't want to be without someone.

"That's a good question," he finally said. "I guess only the two of them can say whether or not it was true love. Why do you ask?"

"Something your mother said to me at the wedding."

"Uh oh," he said. "I should warn you not to put too much stock in what Flo says. She's a shameless matchmaker. In fact it's her fault that Nick and Abby are together today."

"Fault? Interesting choice of words. What did your mother do?" she asked.

"Nick and Ab went to the cabin in the mountains and the only reason she agreed to go with my brother was because she thought the rest of the family was going too and they wouldn't be alone."

"What happened? Did they wind up alone?"

He nodded. "Thanks to Ma. She threatened to send incriminating baby pictures to the local newspaper if any one of us showed our faces in the mountains. She can be pretty determined when she's on a covert mission."

"What did that have to do with Nick and Abby getting together?"

"They needed time alone to fall in love."

"Apparently it worked. You shouldn't be so hard on your mother."

"No?"

She shook her head. "She's a wonderful lady—

strong, loving. Very human. How can you not admire a woman who would do anything for her children?''

"I guess."

"You can't truly appreciate her because you don't know any different. But she gave me a different perspective on relationships. You never told me that your parents were separated for a short time."

That stopped him. A vague discomfort settled over him. A distant memory of a child's pain, fear and confusion. "They split up?"

"That's what your mother told me. You didn't know?"

"I did," he said uncertainly. He thought about it, sorting through his memories, feeling unsettled. Feeling as if his foundation had cracked and his world tilted. "I think I knew. But I was pretty young. I'm not sure if I remember or Nick said something. My parents never talked about it with us. Did she tell you what happened?"

Liz shook her head. "But whatever it was, she took all the blame. The important thing, according to Flo, is love. Two people who have that and the right motivation can make a relationship work. Anyone else shouldn't bother."

"Like your parents?"

"Not exactly. She said staying together in that situation is hard on children. It keeps the wound open and festering. I think she was getting into the milieu of my profession. I like your mom."

"My mother said that your mother gave love a bad name and you're singing her praises?"

"She didn't come right out and say that." Liz shrugged, drawing his attention to the way her T-shirt tantalizingly molded to her breasts. "I've thought about it a lot since talking to Flo. I think my mother was like your friend Bill. She stayed with my father because it was better than being alone. I'm not convinced she actually loved him. But that was her decision. I wouldn't let anyone treat me that way. I'd rather be alone than let someone into my life who would make me unhappy. Maybe your friends are wiser than you think. If they don't have the right stuff to stay together, maybe it's best for them to split up.''

He stared at her. She was certainly singing a different tune. That put him off balance. Not to mention the revived memory of his parents' marital problems. He'd thought their relationship was perfect. They had always given him a lot to live up to. Now he was reminded that there was a time when things weren't so rosy. Where did that leave him?

''Ma missed her calling,'' he said sharply. ''She should hang out a shingle and do family counseling.''

Liz smiled. ''She's wonderful. In fact your whole family is pretty sensational.''

''Really?'' he asked, feeling that familiar twist of jealousy. It was sharper somehow because his whole world was out of whack.

She nodded. ''I talked with Nick and Abby a bit and if I had to bet, I'd lay odds that their marriage will be a good one.''

''I hope so,'' he said cautiously.

''They're so in love you can almost touch the aura that surrounds them when they look at each other,'' she said.

''Abby's good people. Nick is the best. I hope they don't wind up facing a judge to split up the Tupperware.''

She looked at him questioningly. "My, but we're cynical."

"I've been taking lessons from you."

"Well listen up, Mr. Glass-is-half-empty, your parents are cool. Your brothers are fantastic. Very funny and good-looking."

"Is that so?" he said, his jealousy cranking up a notch. He should never have left her alone with Alex and Luke.

"Yes, that's so. But when you look at your parents, it's easy to see where you guys got your good looks and your ethics."

"You don't say."

"Flo and Tom are a handsome couple. They have passed on all the right genes to their offspring."

"Which offspring in particular?" he couldn't help asking.

"Are you fishing for a compliment?" She raised one eyebrow.

"You bet I am."

"Well in my humble opinion, you're the best looking of the lot."

"Thank you."

"But more important than looks is their values. I find it inspirational that they had problems and worked them out because they're really and truly in love."

Joe nodded. "Yeah, like I said, they've set a standard impossible to live up to. And I gave up trying."

She frowned. "I never really believed you meant that."

"Well, believe it. I feel lucky to have found a niche in the cuddlers program."

"Really? Being a cuddler satisfies all your emotional needs?"

He nodded. "Pretty much. It's like the family I'll probably never have. Hasn't it fulfilled those needs for you?"

"I guess," she said. But he got the feeling her heart wasn't in that answer.

Joe got another feeling, that he'd somehow let her down. He didn't much like it. But since he wasn't quite sure what he'd done, or not done, he didn't know how to fix it.

"The program is a good thing," he said reaching in the dark to repair damage. "It's given me a lot of ideas for on-site child care in the restaurants. Not to mention that you and I have become very good friends."

They were more than that, and he knew it. But he wasn't prepared to name it. Love? The idea made him want to hightail it in the other direction. Especially after she'd reminded him of his parents' separation. Not only that, he didn't want to burden Liz with emotional declarations. She had mellowed; he liked what they had. Why rock the boat? Friends was a good safe label, he decided.

"And you're perfectly content with friendship?" she asked, a frown marring the smooth skin of her forehead.

"Absolutely." He nodded.

"I see," she said in a voice that told him she didn't see at all. She pulled her hand from his.

That was bad enough. But it was the shadow of disillusionment and sadness in her eyes that whacked out his world even more.

* * *

Liz straightened the red, white and blue paper tablecloth and napkins covering one of the long tables set up in the cafeteria to hold goodies. She and Essie Martinez had agreed on a Fourth of July motif for the volunteer thank-you reception since the holiday was about a week away. And getting into the milieu of that holiday, Liz thought how Regional Medical Center volunteers were dynamite. One especially tall, dark, and hunky cuddler came immediately to mind.

Followed quickly by a sharp stab of pain.

What had made her think that calling the weird, wild, wacky relationship they shared friendship would spare her the hurt and humiliation of a broken heart? She kicked herself for breaking her self-imposed rules—never be friends with a guy. It gets complicated. Especially when you fall in love with him. Several things had crystallized for her after he'd stopped by to see her the other night. He didn't want more than friendship. He didn't want a serious relationship. He didn't want *her* for anything long term. And in spite of herself, she had fallen head over heels in love with Joe Marchetti.

"Liz?"

She looked up to see Sam standing beside her. Shaking her head slightly to clear it she said, "Hi, Samantha. How long have you been there?"

"Long enough. You were lost in thought. Does it have anything to do with our best looking volunteer whose last name starts with Marchetti?"

"Could be," Liz admitted. "But if you spread that around, I'll deny it."

Sam made a cross over her heart. "No one will hear it from me, boss. Anything I can do to help?"

Liz shook her head. "No help is necessary. We're

just *friends*." Even she heard the bitter emphasis on the word.

"Is there a problem with that?"

Yes. And the devil of it was that she was the one who'd insisted on it. She had no right to be upset because he'd actually listened to her. But right and rational thought went out the window when a catch like Joe Marchetti walked in the front door.

Liz had been foolish enough to think that she was immune to love. How arrogant was that? Now she was facing her worst fear—hook, line, and sinker in love with a guy who wanted to be her pal, buddy, chum.

Now her heart hurt.

She was tempted to go to the hospital's cardiology department and see if there was any treatment for her disorder. But she knew her malady wouldn't show up on any of the tests and there was no medicine she could take to make it better. After a lot of thought during some sleepless nights, she had decided on a prescription for her particular cardiac condition.

"Is there a problem being friends with Joe?" Sam asked again.

Liz met the other woman's gaze and forced herself to focus. This wasn't something she wanted to discuss. She would give her the placebo response. "No problem at all."

"Good." Sam angled her head toward the door. "Because he's here. And he's coming this way."

Liz kept telling herself not to look in his direction even as she turned her head and let her parched spirit drink in the sight of him. She didn't have the will-power to deny herself. Joe had become like nourishment to her soul. Her heart started to pound, her stomach quivered as if a hundred hummingbirds had nested there and were stretching their wings. Worst of all, her legs trembled, threatening to land her on her keister right there in the cafeteria.

He looked so wonderful. That lock of dark hair that tumbled onto his forehead. His big, friendly smile showing straight white teeth that would do his orthodontist proud. His white dress shirt was wrinkled from a day at the office, as were his navy pin-striped slacks. A red-and-blue silk tie hung from his loosened collar, drawing her attention to his wide, muscled chest.

Liz shivered. She knew the sensation of being held in his arms, clasped against that stalwart chest. She knew the feel of his powerful body cradling hers. And the magic of his kiss. She had expected to regret all those sensations. Instead, she was grateful to have such heart-stopping memories.

Like the fragrance of his aftershave. It surrounded her now, as he stopped beside her. "Hello, ladies."

"Hi, Joe," Sam said. "I've got to go."

He gave her a look of mock hurt. "That's not very good for my self-esteem. I show up. You split."

Liz wasn't as worried about his feelings as she was being alone with him. "Where are you off to in such a hurry, Sam?"

"Back to O.B. I'm on duty. They sent me down to steal some sweets. The plunder of choice would be chocolate."

Liz laughed, even though her heart cried out not to be left to face Joe by herself. "You know there's always too much at these functions. Take a big plate up to the staff."

Sam saluted. "Yes'm."

Then her friend was gone and Joe smiled at her.

Liz's heart swelled with love at the same time squeezing tight with pain. If only he could care about her the way she wanted him to. She wished she had a do-over. Maybe if she hadn't been so hard on him when he first volunteered. But hindsight was twenty-twenty. There was no use crying over tossed zingers. She'd tried to protect herself. It hadn't worked. She glanced up at his handsome, smiling face. Who knew there weren't enough weapons in the world to protect herself from Mr. Wonderful?

"So," Joe said, looking down at her.

"So," she answered. She rocked back on her heels and clasped her hands behind her back. "Help yourself to some coffee and dessert. After that the Director of Volunteer Services for the hospital is going to give out certificates of appreciation." She started to walk away, to lose herself in the crowd of volunteers steadily arriving to fill up the room.

"Hey." He frowned at her.

"What?"

"Where are you going? I've been looking forward to seeing you all day."

Liz's heart soared at his words. Then she reminded herself it was only in friendship. Like the night he'd dropped by her house because he was bummed about his divorcing friend. She had to stop expecting more. There was only one way she could think of to do that.

"Joe, I have to mingle with everyone. You're not the only cuddler in the program."

Just the only cuddler she loved.

His forehead puckered as his eyebrows drew together. He stuck his hands in the pockets of his slacks. "I'm sensing something here. A disturbance. What put a knot in your stethoscope?"

She looked around at the people filling the cafeteria. "I don't think this is the right place to discuss it."

"So there really is something bothering you. I was hoping I was wrong."

"No, you're not wrong." She was surprised that he'd sized her mood up so quickly. Her close girlfriends could do that. But since she'd never had a guy *friend* before, she'd figured she could hide her feelings from him. "But I can't talk about it here— Oh!"

He reached out suddenly, taking her arm and steering her toward a back door that led to an outside patio. They left the air-conditioned cafeteria for the balmy summer night air.

When the self-closing door slammed shut, Joe looked down at her and said, "Now we're alone. So tell me what's wrong."

Liz briefly toyed with the idea of shining him on, then quickly eighty-sixed that. She was no coward. Honesty. That was always the best policy. She'd learned that was one of Joe's most wonderful qualities—his straightforward, aboveboard way of dealing with life. She wouldn't give him less.

"You said you'd looked forward to seeing me all day. That's what's wrong. I don't want you to do that anymore. And please don't drop by my house."

"What are you saying?" There was an angry edge to his voice that didn't make sense—unless he cared. But that was impossible.

"I'm saying that I can't see you anymore. I'd appreciate it if you don't seek me out either here at the hospital, or outside of it."

"Why? I don't understand."

"We want different things."

"What are we talking here? Cars? Movies? What?" His tone was clipped, irritated.

"For starters, you want friendship. I want the brass ring, not second place."

"I'm second place?"

"You're twisting my words," she said.

He looked stunned. "I don't think so. You're the one who insisted on friendship. I don't get it—"

"When you put it like that, I guess it doesn't make a lot of sense. But I realized that I want the whole ball of wax. In the long run I think separating would be for the best."

"For who?" he asked.

"Both of us I think." She sighed. "I realized I want to find the fairy tale and you stopped believing in it."

"But to end a beautiful friendship—why, Liz?"

"Before someone gets hurt," she said, proud that she kept her voice steady.

"This is nuts. Have you been out in the sun too long without a hat? What have I ever done to make you distrust me?" he demanded. He jammed his hand through his hair as he loomed over her looking furious. "I would never hurt you," he said, jabbing his finger in the air to punctuate each word.

You already have, she said to herself. She could almost hear the sound of her heart cracking. He couldn't give her more than friendship. He couldn't give her what he'd made her see that she wanted. He couldn't give her love. To see him knowing he could never return her feelings would repeat her mother's mistake. He'd made her face her cynicism and tuck it away. She was grateful for that. But she wouldn't give love a bad name.

She put her hand on his forearm, the part bared by his rolled up sleeve. The muscles contracted beneath her fingers. She felt the warmth of his skin one last time, and was grateful that he didn't pull away.

"I believe you would never deliberately hurt me," she clarified.

"What does that mean?" he asked sharply. "Why are you suddenly changing the rules?"

She shook her head unwilling to explain that everything had changed when she'd realized she loved him and he would never return that feeling. "There's really no point in discussing this further. Let's not say anything we'll regret."

"I already regret what you said," he practically growled.

"Let's just say goodbye," she pleaded.

She knew it was a mistake, but she couldn't resist the urge to kiss him one last time. She stood up on tiptoe, her intention to press her lips to his cheek.

At the last second, he turned his face and captured her mouth with his.

Chapter Eleven

Joe slid his arm around her waist and pulled her to him. Adrenaline fueled by anger mixed with a healthy dose of testosterone roared through him. One good kiss would fix everything. It would show her that she couldn't say goodbye.

He cupped the back of her head with his other hand, making the contact of their mouths more firm. With his tongue, he easily coaxed her lips apart, and slipped into the honeyed recess of her mouth. Her sigh of satisfaction followed by a moan of surrender filled him with triumph. She cared about him. He knew it. This would change her mind.

He nibbled small kisses at each corner of her mouth and her breathing quickened, matching his own. He teased his way across her jaw and found the spot just below her ear, the place he knew would make her jump when he lavished attention there. She arched closer to him, as if she couldn't get near enough, as if she wanted to dissolve into him. He would bet everything he owned that she'd forgotten that baloney about splitting up.

He ran his knuckles down her soft cheek as she slipped her hand up his chest and curved her palm around his neck.

Joe smiled against her mouth. "So much for not seeing each other anymore," he said.

When Liz stiffened in his arms, he knew he'd made a mistake and more than anything wished he had the power to call the words back. Again, he wasn't sure what he'd done wrong. Confusion didn't begin to describe how he felt. He just knew that when she'd said they had to stop seeing each other, it was as if someone had dropped a boulder on his chest. He wanted time with her. Promises of happy ever after were something else.

She pushed against his chest. "Let me go."

"Liz, please—"

She shook her head. "No. This was a mistake."

"That's not what the little moaning noises you made were saying."

"I mean it, Joe. I can't do this. Please, let me go," she whispered desperately.

He lowered his hands to his sides, but it was several moments before she backed up a step, still breathing hard, he noticed. So was he. It took all his willpower *not* to pull her back against him. One more kiss would convince her that she couldn't stop seeing him. Her decision was a momentary lapse, brain freeze, overwork pushing her into a rash decision. He wanted to go on just as they had been. Hanging out. Talking. See where they went from there. Why did she have to make things complicated?

"Liz, I don't get this." He ran a shaking hand

through his hair. "Why now?" he asked harshly. "I worked my tail off to convince you I'm on the up-and-up. That I'm nothing like your father. You even said I'm a swell guy. This makes no sense."

"You showed me that I can have it all, but not with you. All we can be is friends."

He nodded. "We're good as friends. I like having you in my life."

"I'm an all-or-nothing kind of woman, Joe. That's my flaw." She folded her arms across her waist in a protective gesture. "Second best is first loser. I'm taking myself out of the game."

"You couldn't kiss me like that and possibly mean that you don't want to see me anymore."

She touched her fingers to lips swollen from his kiss. "I meant every word I said."

"But you kissed me back."

"Maybe. I'm sorry. I didn't mean to." She dragged in a big breath. "I meant to kiss you g-goodbye."

"Okay, I get that I'm second best. But I don't understand this all-or-nothing attitude."

She met his gaze, her eyes pleading. "Joe, please don't make this harder. I've made up my mind."

He suddenly got it. She really did mean to say goodbye. There was nothing he could do to change her mind. Hurt and anger gave way to frustration and fury as he felt himself losing the battle to keep her in his life.

He paced back and forth for several moments. Then he stopped in front of her and looked down. "You made up your mind about me that day I gave you my volunteer form. No matter what I did, it wouldn't have been enough."

She lifted her hand toward him. "Joe, please—"

"I've got a piece of advice for you, Nurse Ratchett. Next time a guy walks into your office, let him know he needs wings, and a halo. And if he wants to be your friend, warn him that he needs to walk on water, too."

Anger, frustration, and fury disappeared as pain exploded inside him. In his whole life, he'd never felt anything close to this crushing desolation.

He would never let her see it. Without another word, he turned and walked away.

"You ask him."

"Do I have stupid tattooed across my forehead?" Luke asked his brother Alex. "You ask him."

Sitting on the chaise by his parents' pool, Joe opened one eye when he realized he couldn't ignore the two of them. When had his brothers become so irritating? Normally they all got along well.

"Go away," Joe practically growled.

"We can't." Alex sat on the lounge across from him.

"Sure you can. About-face and put one foot in front of the other until you're gone. Easy."

Luke pulled up a chair. "Ma sent us out here. The only thing worse than bringing up this subject with you would be facing her without the information we were dispatched to obtain."

"And what information would that be?" Joe nearly snarled. As if he didn't know.

He also knew he was acting like a jerk, but couldn't seem to help it. Why had he let his mother talk him into coming over for a Fourth of July barbecue? He wasn't fit company for man or beast. Black didn't come close to describing his mood. And every day had been the same, ever since that night last week when Liz gave him the heave-ho.

"What the hell's wrong with you?" Luke demanded.

"That's for me to know and you to find out," Joe automatically answered.

His response was so rooted in childhood, he felt about ten years old again. And he hadn't felt this miserable since his older brother had taken away his yo-yo. But he was a man now. Nick was happily married. And Liz had taken away something far more precious than a toy.

Joe knew that he would never find the happiness that Nick and Abby had. Not without Liz. But she'd made it clear as the water in the pool that they were kaput. The knot of pain he'd carried around since that night tightened a notch. He closed his eyes behind his sunglasses.

"Well, bro, I guess it's time to bring in the big guns." The voice was Alex's.

"Ma," both of them said together.

Joe heard their retreating footsteps. He was tempted to hightail it through the back gate. But not only was that the chicken way out, there was a part of him that suspected *this* was why he'd accepted his mother's invitation. He needed to talk to someone.

A few minutes later, he heard the click of sandals on the pool deck. Then the corner of his chaise dipped.

"Joseph, what's all this nonsense? How many times have I told you—if you can't say anything nice, don't say anything at all?"

"They asked for it, Ma. Guys know when to back off. Luke and Alex should know better."

"So are you going to bite my head off too?"

"No."

"I'm not sure one syllable answers are an improvement, Joseph Paul."

Uh-oh. Both of his names. He opened his eyes and sat up straighter on the lounge, making more room for her. "What do you want from me, Ma?"

"I want to know what you did to Liz."

That did it. He pushed his sunglasses to the top of his head and glared at her. "What makes you think *I* did something to her?" he asked.

"Because I had a long and very satisfying heart-to-heart with her at the wedding."

"Yeah. I've been meaning to talk to you about that." It was right after the wedding that Liz said she couldn't see him anymore. Had his own mother sabotaged him?

Flo pointed at him. "I know for a fact that she's deeply in love with you."

He stared at her. "She's got a funny way of showing it."

"You have to cut her some slack. She told me about her family life, her father's infidelity and her one unsuccessful relationship. But I know I got through to her. I know I convinced her that love was worth taking a chance."

"So this is all your fault." He felt the muscle in his jaw contract as he gritted his teeth.

"Define 'this' and I'll let you know whether or not I'll accept responsibility."

"Liz told me she can't see me anymore. She said she won't settle for second best because she wants the brass ring."

"Good for her," Flo said approvingly.

He looked at his mother as if she'd lost her mind. "Since when am I second best?"

"Did you tell her how you feel about her?" she asked, ignoring his question.

"Everything was hunky-dory between us until you got hold of her," he said, hedging. "What the hell did you say to her?"

"Don't swear, dear."

"Sorry. But things were fine between us. Great in fact. She'd never been so relaxed with me."

Flo pumped her arm. "I knew I got through to her."

"Then why did she dump me?"

"You must have done something. What did you say to her between the wedding and the dumping?"

"Me? What makes you think I said something?"

"Because you're a man, dear. You can't help it."

"I do human resources for a living, Ma. I've learned how to help it."

"You've never been in love before. That tends to make a man's brain useless. But other parts of his body pick up the slack for—you know."

That was a place he didn't want to go. Not with his mother. Talking about "you know" with the support group moms was one thing. But discussing his libido, especially where Liz was concerned, with his mother was quite another.

"Male bashing is a cheap shot," he said. "And I'm your son. How can you take Liz's side over mine?"

"I'm not taking sides, dear. I'm just putting on my diplomat hat and trying to get to the bottom of who fired the first shot. She was fine at the wedding. I've never seen her more beautiful. I know her heart was lighter after we talked. And my love radar can't be that far off. She is putty in your hands. Or she should be. What happened?''

He thought for a moment. "I stopped by her place the day I went to court with Bill."

"Your friend who's going through a divorce," she said.

He nodded. "Liz and I talked about it. I told her I was glad that we'd become such good friends."

Flo groaned. "Tell me you didn't say that."

"She was going on about love and family. How devoted you and Dad are. I agreed. You've set a standard impossible to follow. I gave up trying. Friends are better."

She groaned again. "I see the problem. As soon as Liz let down her guard, you put yours up. You shot yourself in the foot, dear. And I have a sneaking suspicion you did it on purpose."

Now he was getting irritated. He was the *dumpee!* He'd never hurt so much in his life. His world fell apart. Why was it his fault? He remembered Liz mentioning his parents' separation. "Would you like to tell me about you and Dad splitting up when I was a kid?"

Flo stiffened beside him and he wanted to take back the words. She sighed. "I didn't think you remembered."

"Just a little. It's more like a dream."

"A nightmare," she said. "And yes, I would like to tell you about it. For starters, it's all my fault."

"How?"

She hesitated for so long he thought she wasn't going to say anything. Finally she squared her shoulders and took a deep breath. "I was unfaithful."

That stunned him. He wasn't sure he wanted to hear any more. "Ma, you don't have to talk about this—"

"It's time I did. Your father and I thought it best to never bring up this painful subject. Now I see that decision may have cost you."

"I don't get it," he said shaking his head. "This is dumb—"

"I turned to another man, Joe. It was brief. Not that that makes it all right. But it was a time when I had three small, active boys. Your father was hardly ever home. He worked so hard to build the restaurant, then expand the business." She swallowed hard and shook her head. "I don't mean to make excuses. I'm just trying to make you understand how it was. I was married, but I felt as if I was alone. I'd never been so lonely."

"I don't know what to say, Ma."

"There's nothing to say. It was between your father and I. He moved out of the house."

"I remember. I don't think I'd ever seen you cry before." That was why he remembered. Young as he'd been, seeing his mother break down was like watching the Rock of Gibraltar shatter into a zillion pieces.

She nodded. "You were the only one who saw me break down. Luke and Rosie weren't born yet. Alex was too little to remember. And Nick wanted to know when his daddy would be home from his business trip. But seeing the fear on your little face—" Her voice cracked and she stopped, struggling to control herself. She shook her head once and said, "It was the worst thing I ever went through. And the best."

"The best?" He blinked. "Now you've lost me."

"Dad and I realized how much we missed and loved each other. He came back and we made promises to spend time together, to nurture the relationship. Unfortunately we also vowed never to talk about that time with each other, or to you boys. I see now that was wrong."

"Why?"

"Think about it, Joe. You have never let yourself fall in love. For years you've boasted about your father and I and thirty-five years of perfect happiness."

"You and Dad *have* been happy for thirty-five years."

She shook her head. "We've been together. But not always happy. There were more good times than bad. But it wasn't perfect. There's no such thing. It's time you faced that."

"Did you love him, Ma? The other guy?" Joe wasn't sure how he felt about this. But he needed to know the answer to that question.

She sighed. "I don't know whether or not you'll believe this, but the honest answer is—no. I respected and admired him. I liked him. He said he loved me, wanted me to marry him. I was tempted, but I couldn't do it."

"Why not?"

"Because I knew your father was the love of my life, and always would be. In spite of that awful time, I would marry Tom Marchetti again in a heartbeat. I'm profoundly appreciative of the bad times."

"That doesn't make sense, Ma," he said, an edge to his voice. He wasn't sure how to feel about what she was telling him. Should he be angry? Mad at her for hurting his father?

"It makes perfect sense. If not for the bad, we

would take the relationship for granted. That separation brought us closer together, it made us treasure the good times."

He shook his head. "I don't know what to say, Ma."

"It's okay, dear." She put her hand on his arm. "I can discuss it calmly because it all happened many years ago. But you're just finding out about it."

"Does anyone else know?"

She shook her head. "I won't swear you to secrecy. If you feel the need to share it with your brothers or your sister, you have my permission. Because I have the feeling that your childhood memory of that time left a scar we didn't know was there."

He studied her, the way her silver hair shone in the sunlight. The lines around her eyes and mouth were deeper, and he could see the toll confessing her indiscretion had taken. He still wasn't quite sure what this had to do with him, what "scar" she was talking about, but she'd felt he needed to know and it had been hard on her. He loved her for that.

"You and Dad are really okay now?" he asked.

She thought about his question and smiled, erasing the tension. "We're friends, confidants, lovers—"

"Don't go there, Ma."

She laughed. "We're better than okay." Her expression, her words, convinced him that the foundation of the family was sound. "But you're not."

"I'll get over it."

"Running from love has been your pattern your whole adult life. It's time to dig your heels in. Stand and fight for the woman you love. Snap out of your comfort zone. That's why I brought up all this ancient history. I want to see you with someone who is the

love of your life for the bad times and the good.''
She met his gaze. ''I would bet my membership in
the romance-of-the-month book club your someone is
Liz.''

Anger and hurt swirled inside him because Liz
would never be his. But he couldn't help asking,
''Why do you think she's the one?''

''The cuddlers program.''

''You know about that?'' he asked, surprised.

''Rosie told me. It's clear to both of us that after
meeting Liz you couldn't forget her. Volunteering
was a way to get to know her better, to get close to
her.''

He shook his head. ''She doesn't agree.''

''Change her mind.'' The voice she used was one
he remembered from childhood, when one of them
had done something wrong.

It was a tone he learned never to ignore. ''I'll try,''
he said.

Flo shook her head disapprovingly. ''Second place
attitude. Not the mind-set of a man determined to win
the woman he loves.''

She sounded like Liz—second place is first loser.

For the first time since he'd walked out on Liz, a
grin threatened. ''You are one tough cookie, Ma.''

She smiled. ''I had to be, dear. Motherhood isn't
for wimps.''

''Okay. I'll change her mind.''

''How?''

''Boy, you don't give up, do you?''

''Never, and neither should you.''

''I'm not sure how I'll get through to her. But I
will not give up until I have achieved my objective.''

''Well done, dear.''

Chapter Twelve

"**Y**ou're looking like the eighth dwarf, Crabby."

Liz looked up from the paperwork on her desk to see Sam in the doorway. "Don't let the frown fool you. Inside I'm doing the dance of joy."

"And I'm a supermodel moonlighting as a baby nurse." Sam put a hand on her hip. "This wouldn't have anything to do with our star male volunteer and your friendship status, would it?" Before Liz could deny it, Sam held up her hand and said, "The truth please."

Liz sighed and leaned back in her chair, trying to keep the pain from filtering through her defenses. She linked her fingers and settled her hands on her abdomen. It was support-group night and she had on her navy suit, the same outfit she'd worn when Joe had charmed all those tired, overworked, new moms. Not to mention one tired, overworked assistant supervising baby nurse.

"Okay. The truth is I miss Joe." A sharp stab of pain hit her somewhere in the region of her heart.

"Why? He's here all the time. He hasn't welshed on a volunteer shift. In fact, half the time he shows up in the middle of the night. I don't know when the man sleeps."

Me, either, Liz thought, worrying about him. Had his insomnia flared up? Did it have anything to do with the fact that she was on his mind? That idea did make her heart do a little two-step before she warned herself not to hope. More important than any of that, was he getting enough rest? That worried her the most. It could be dangerous.

"How does he look?" Liz couldn't help asking.

"Like the ninth dwarf, Cranky," Sam answered. "What happened between you two that night? The truth please," she said again.

"You are almost as cynical as I am," Liz complained. "I told him that it would be best if we didn't spend time together anymore."

"What would make you say something like that?"

"He only wants friendship."

"He said that?"

"Pretty much," Liz answered.

"And you believe him?"

"I have no reason not to. I learned the hard way that Joe Marchetti doesn't lie."

Sam shook her head in disgust. "I have never seen two people more determined to ignore the obvious."

"And that would be?"

"You guys are crazy about each other."

"Make that singular. I'm nuts about him. He doesn't feel the same way."

"I think you're wrong about that."

"Then why does he just want to be friends?"

"There could be lots of reasons," Sam said moving into the room. "He's playing it slow and cautious. Doesn't want to scare you off. Or he's relationship-shy for some reason. But in my humble opinion, the diagnosis for what ails you two is l-o-v-e."

Time to change the subject, Liz thought. No way would she get her hopes up. "You didn't come all the way to my office to counsel me in the finer points of l-o-v-e. What brought you here, Sam?"

Her friend gave her a look that told her she knew that was an evasive maneuver. "I want to put in a request for a weekend off before you do the schedule."

"Okay." Liz wrote down the date. "That shouldn't be a problem. Anything else? I have the support group in a few minutes."

Sam shook her head. "Nothing except try not to let your wounded pride stand in the way of your happiness."

"Wouldn't dream of it," Liz said. But she also knew that only a moron would beat her head against a brick wall. Joe didn't want more than friendship. He didn't feel the same way about her as she did about him. Breaking it off had been the best thing for her.

"Thanks, Sam."

"Any time."

Then she was alone. A wave of loneliness washed over her, brought about, no doubt, by talking about Joe. Most of the time she managed to stay busy enough to keep him on the periphery of her thoughts. But every once in a while, a memory would invade, so vivid, and so painful that it took her breath away.

She could only hope that time would dull her feelings. But she had a terrible hunch that he was the only man who would ever make her heart pound and her knees weak.

She'd had one chance. Joe Marchetti was her brass ring and she'd missed it.

She got up from her desk and went to the window behind it, looking out over the landscaped front of the hospital. At least she had a career she loved. Not everyone got to have it all—love, family, and a great job. No doubt she was destined to be married to her job. The thought produced another piercing pain around her heart.

"Liz?"

Joe! That wonderful voice—deep, husky, warm as fine brandy—took her breath away. How she'd missed him. She put a hand on the wall to steady herself. Then she turned around.

"Hi," she said. "Can I help you?"

"I hope so."

He stood there in her doorway looking sexy and handsome, and tempting as sin. In his dress shirt, with tie at half staff and wrinkled, gray pinstriped slacks he looked like a *GQ* model after a hard day at the office.

"What is it?"

"I came here to tell you that you were right."

She blinked. Did he mean she'd been right to say they shouldn't see each other? The thought hurt even though it had been her idea. "About what?" she asked.

"When I joined the cuddlers program, you implied that my motives had something to do with meeting women. You were right."

"I was?"

He nodded. "But it was only one woman and her name was Liz Anderson." His brown eyes were full of sincerity and his dark hair looked as if he'd run his hand through it countless times. "I met her when my niece was born and I never forgot her." He rubbed his ear. "Tug on my ear and I'll follow you anywhere."

Liz was afraid to believe. "Joe, I—"

He held up a hand. "Hear me out. The least you can do is let me explain. I had a long talk with my mom."

"About their split?" she couldn't help asking.

He nodded. "And how it affected me. She said I'd been running from commitment all my life."

Liz laughed and shook her head sadly. "Aren't we a matched set of dysfunctionals?"

"You're missing the point."

"I am?"

"Yes. I've been making excuses to avoid getting involved. I'd seen my mother cry when my dad left. Then I buried the bad stuff but it was always there."

"See, I was right. Your mom should hang out her counseling shingle."

"You were right about something else, too."

"I was?" she asked, stunned.

He nodded. "You and I continuing to see each other as just friends, that would have been a big mistake."

The knife in her heart twisted. Who knew being right could hurt so much? Struggling to keep her voice steady she said, "A mistake?"

"Yeah. Because friendship doesn't exactly describe how I feel about you. I'm in l—"

"Holy cow!" she said, looking at her watch. "I'm late for group." She walked past him, toward the door.

"Liz, wait. I've got to tell you—"

She shook her head. "It's hard enough for new moms to get anywhere on time. The least I can do is not keep them waiting."

She made it into the hallway and hurried toward classroom 2. In spite of all her self-warnings hope blossomed in her heart. Sam could be right. She should stop ignoring the obvious. She was crazy about Joe Marchetti. She should get over her fear of falling and go after what she wanted. She would do that right after she fulfilled her obligation to the support group.

"What just happened?" Joe said to the empty room. "No way am I waiting."

He went after her. He'd prepared himself to fight the good fight. He'd known it wouldn't be easy to win her. But he hadn't expected to compete with her job. Well, dammit, he couldn't wait until her meeting was over. He'd been living in hell ever since Liz had dumped him. He couldn't stand it anymore. He wanted things settled between them once and for all. If he had to do it in front of God and the new mothers' support group, then so be it. But one way or the other, he was going to fix things.

There were only four moms with babies in the room. At least that worked in his favor. He recognized Andie and Barbara and their respective offspring. The other two women were strangers.

"Liz, before you start, I want to settle things between you and I."

"This isn't the time or place."

"I'm sorry about that." He turned to the moms. "I apologize for bursting in like this, but Liz and I have some issues."

"Romantic issues?" Andie adjusted her nursing baby.

"Yes," he said.

"Then go right ahead," she said. "You guys are more entertaining than my soap opera."

Liz looked at the woman and shook her head. "I was counting on you ladies for backup."

Barbara tossed a strand of long blond hair over her shoulder. "He looks determined, Liz. Might as well get it over with. You know how men are when they get that whole focus thing going."

"Actually, no," Liz said.

"Then let me show you," Joe said. "I want you in my life—"

"Now there's focus," she said wryly. "In your life? As what? Friends? We've already gone through this. You're a confirmed bachelor."

"I was a little hasty about that," he admitted. "I had a long talk with Ma—"

"Uh-oh," Andie said. "You're not a mama's boy are you?"

"Of course not," he scoffed. "But she explained some things that happened when I was a kid, a situation I hardly even remembered." He glanced at the women watching him intently. No way would he air dirty laundry in front of them. He respected his parents too much. They'd put it behind them. Once he'd explained to the woman he loved why he'd messed up, they would put it behind them, too.

He turned back to Liz. "Ma said she talked to you about it at the wedding."

She nodded. "I remember."

"It stuck with me. That situation made a negative imprint on an impressionable young boy. And along with the less than successful relationships I've seen, well I guess you could say it all made me gun-shy."

"You were so adamant about giving up on finding what your folks have. Why should I believe that you've changed your mind?" Liz challenged.

"Because I'm looking at things differently now. I know there's no such thing as a perfect relationship—"

"You can say that again," Andie interjected.

He grinned at the woman, then looked back at Liz. What was she thinking? Was he getting through to her? He couldn't tell by the expression on her face. But so far her comments made him apprehensive that the same moxie that had attracted him to her in the first place would work against him now.

He met her gaze, willing her to believe him. "It takes work to be a couple. I'm ready, willing and able to do what it takes to make a successful relationship with you, Liz."

"I don't know," she said, shaking her head. "You were so set on staying *friends*—"

Barbara groaned. "He didn't give you that speech, did he? The old it's getting too serious, let's just stay friends line?"

"I did not," he defended himself. He pointed to Liz. "She was the one who insisted on the friends label."

"Liz, what were you thinking?" a brunette holding a sleeping baby asked.

Liz looked at her. "Jessica, it wasn't like that. Getting serious scared me because of what happened in

my family. I didn't want to get in over my head."
She glanced at the moms, then looked at Joe. "But I
couldn't help it."

Joe knew she was weakening. He held up his hand.
"I solemnly swear, in front of this new mothers' support group, that I will never be unfaithful to you."

"I think he means it," chimed in a redhead, standing so she could bounce her baby.

"It's just not that simple," Liz said.

Time for reinforcements. Joe turned to the moms.
"Help me out here. Why won't she see me anymore?
Why won't she listen to me?"

"Maybe you're not saying what she needs to
hear," Andie said.

"Such as?" Joe shot back.

Andie shifted the infant in her arms. "That you
love her. That you can't live without her. That you
want to marry her." She looked at Liz. "Well? Has
he said any of that?"

"Nope," she confirmed. "He's done none of the
above."

"All right." He went down on one knee in front
of all of them. He took Liz's hand and had the satisfaction of knowing that she was shaking, too. He
met her gaze. "Liz, this is a tough room. They want
flowery declarations and I'll do my best, but the bottom line is, and it's the honest truth, I love you. I've
missed you. I'm a mess without you. Will you do me
the honor of spending the next fifty years with me?
Will you marry me?"

Her eyes filled with tears. "Joe, I—" She stopped
and swallowed hard, shaking her head.

"Anyone can see that he loves you," Barbara said.
"Liz, you'd be a fool to turn him down."

Liz nodded. "You're right. And I've been the world's biggest fool." She met Joe's gaze. "I was afraid when you would only commit to friendship. I had to pull back from you to protect myself. I know you're telling me the truth about loving me."

Relief filtered through the tension he'd carried with him all day. "How do you know?"

"It's in your kiss." She pulled him to his feet. "Now it's my turn. I need to tell you how much I love you."

She took his face in her hands and drew it down and stood on tiptoe. Touching her lips to his in a tender, truthful, heartfelt demonstration of her love, she sighed against his mouth. He wrapped his arms around her and deepened the communication.

When they came up for air, Joe looked around and noticed that they were alone. "I busted up your group. I'm sorry."

"I'm not." She grinned at him. "What do you want to bet they're going home to do 'you know' with some husbands who will be happy men?"

"I'd be a happier man if you would explain to me why you could be so relaxed with my brothers and I had to work so hard to make you admit I'm a swell guy."

"I always thought you were Mr. Wonderful. But I wasn't attracted to Luke or Alex. They couldn't hurt me the way you could."

He tightened his hold on her. "I'd never hurt you. I'm not your father."

"I know," she said nodding. "And I'm not my mother. I'm a strong, independent woman who can handle whatever curves are thrown at me." She smiled up at him. "I realized something when I talked to your mother at the wedding."

"If it's good, I owe Ma even more than I thought."

"I realized that I love you. So when you did your spin about friendship, I thought you were telling me you could never love me back. It hurt too much to see you under those circumstances so I broke it off. Although it was impossible, I had to try and get over you so that I could find someone to love me back. You made me see that I wanted that. Thanks for not giving up on me."

"You're welcome. And I'm sorry I put you through that. I'll try to never be that stupid again."

"You're the smartest, most wonderful guy I know," she said, her gaze making him feel as if he could walk on water. She took a deep breath. "And your mom also made me see that if I deny myself love and a relationship, my father wins."

"We can't let that happen." He looked at her and willed her to know how very much he loved her. "And I know a way to make us the winners."

"I'm all ears," she said.

He laughed, then his humor drained away. "I know you think I'm second best, but that will only make me work harder. I would be the happiest man in the world if you say you'll marry me, Liz."

"I'll marry you," she said without hesitation. "And you're not second best. You're my brass ring, Joe Marchetti."

"And you're my happy ever after, Liz Anderson. And, by the way, as soon as it's humanly possible your last name will be Marchetti."

"I can hardly wait." She tilted her head and slid him a sassy look. "So you really care about me?"

"From the first time I saw you."

"How do I know it's love?" she asked.

"It's in my kiss," he answered, knowing what she wanted.

He touched his lips to hers. Without words, he told her of the love that was in his heart. For the next fifty years, he planned to communicate his feelings to her on a very regular basis.

*   *   *   *   *

Look for talented author
Teresa Southwick's next irresistible
tale of love and happily
ever after in the exciting new
Silhouette Romance miniseries,

STORKVILLE, USA,

coming late 2000.

MONTANA MAVERICKS
Big Sky Brides

Legendary love comes to Whitehorn, Montana, once more as beloved authors

Christine Rimmer, Jennifer Greene and Cheryl St.John

present three brand-new stories in this exciting anthology!

Meet the Brennan women:

SUZANNA, DIANA and ISABELLE

Strong-willed beauties who find unexpected love in these irresistible marriage of covnenience stories.

Don't miss
MONTANA MAVERICKS: BIG SKY BRIDES
On sale in February 2000,
only from Silhouette Books!

Available at your favorite retail outlet.

Silhouette ®

PSMMBSB

SILHOUETTE'S 20TH ANNIVERSARY CONTEST
OFFICIAL RULES
NO PURCHASE NECESSARY TO ENTER

1. To enter, follow directions published in the offer to which you are responding. Contest begins 1/1/00 and ends on 8/24/00 (the "Promotion Period"). Method of entry may vary. Mailed entries must be postmarked by 8/24/00, and received by 8/31/00.

2. During the Promotion Period, the Contest may be presented via the Internet. Entry via the Internet may be restricted to residents of certain geographic areas that are disclosed on the Web site. To enter via the Internet, if you are a resident of a geographic area in which Internet entry is permissible, follow the directions displayed on-line, including typing your essay of 100 words or fewer telling us "Where In The World Your Love Will Come Alive." On-line entries must be received by 11:59 p.m. Eastern Standard time on 8/24/00. Limit one e-mail entry per person, household and e-mail address per day, per presentation. If you are a resident of a geographic area in which entry via the Internet is permissible, you may, in lieu of submitting an entry on-line, enter by mail, by hand-printing your name, address, telephone number and contest number/name on an 8"x 11" plain piece of paper and telling us in 100 words or fewer "Where In The World Your Love Will Come Alive," and mailing via first-class mail to: Silhouette 20th Anniversary Contest, (in the U.S.) P.O. Box 9069, Buffalo, NY 14269-9069; (In Canada) P.O. Box 637, Fort Erie, Ontario, Canada L2A 5X3. Limit one 8"x 11" mailed entry per person, household and e-mail address per day. On-line and/or 8"x 11" mailed entries received from persons residing in geographic areas in which Internet entry is not permissible will be disqualified. No liability is assumed for lost, late, incomplete, inaccurate, nondelivered or misdirected mail, or misdirected e-mail, for technical, hardware or software failures of any kind, lost or unavailable network connection, or failed, incomplete, garbled or delayed computer transmission or any human error which may occur in the receipt or processing of the entries in the contest.

3. Essays will be judged by a panel of members of the Silhouette editorial and marketing staff based on the following criteria:

     Sincerity (believability, credibility)—50%

     Originality (freshness, creativity)—30%

     Aptness (appropriateness to contest ideas)—20%

   Purchase or acceptance of a product offer does not improve your chances of winning. In the event of a tie, duplicate prizes will be awarded.

4. All entries become the property of Harlequin Enterprises Ltd., and will not be returned. Winner will be determined no later than 10/31/00 and will be notified by mail. Grand Prize winner will be required to sign and return Affidavit of Eligibility within 15 days of receipt of notification. Noncompliance within the time period may result in disqualification and an alternative winner may be selected. All municipal, provincial, federal, state and local laws and regulations apply. Contest open only to residents of the U.S. and Canada who are 18 years of age or older, and is void wherever prohibited by law. Internet entry is restricted solely to residents of those geographical areas in which Internet entry is permissible. Employees of Torstar Corp., their affiliates, agents and members of their immediate families are not eligible. Taxes on the prizes are the sole responsibility of winners. Entry and acceptance of any prize offered constitutes permission to use winner's name, photograph or other likeness for the purposes of advertising, trade and promotion on behalf of Torstar Corp. without further compensation to the winner, unless prohibited by law. Torstar Corp and D.L. Blair, Inc., their parents, affiliates and subsidiaries, are not responsible for errors in printing or electronic presentation of contest or entries. In the event of printing or other errors which may result in unintended prize values or duplication of prizes, all affected contest materials or entries shall be null and void. If for any reason the Internet portion of the contest is not capable of running as planned, including infection by computer virus, bugs, tampering, unauthorized intervention, fraud, technical failures, or any other causes beyond the control of Torstar Corp. which corrupt or affect the administration, secrecy, fairness, integrity or proper conduct of the contest, Torstar Corp. reserves the right, at its sole discretion, to disqualify any individual who tampers with the entry process and to cancel, terminate, modify or suspend the contest or the Internet portion thereof. In the event of a dispute regarding an on-line entry, the entry will be deemed submitted by the authorized holder of the e-mail account submitted at the time of entry. Authorized account holder is defined as the natural person who is assigned to an e-mail address by an Internet access provider, on-line service provider or other organization that is responsible for arranging e-mail address for the domain associated with the submitted e-mail address.

5. Prizes: Grand Prize—a $10,000 vacation to anywhere in the world. Travelers (at least one must be 18 years of age or older) or parent or guardian if one traveler is a minor, must sign and return a Release of Liability prior to departure. Travel must be completed by December 31, 2001, and is subject to space and accommodations availability. Two hundred (200) Second Prizes—a two-book limited edition autographed collector set from one of the Silhouette Anniversary authors: Nora Roberts, Diana Palmer, Linda Howard or Annette Broadrick (value $10.00 each set). All prizes are valued in U.S. dollars.

6. For a list of winners (available after 10/31/00), send a self-addressed, stamped envelope to: Harlequin Silhouette 20th Anniversary Winners, P.O. Box 4200, Blair, NE 68009-4200.

Contest sponsored by Torstar Corp., P.O. Box 9042, Buffalo, NY 14269-9042.

ENTER FOR
A CHANCE TO WIN*

Silhouette's 20th Anniversary Contest

Tell Us Where in the World
You Would Like *Your* Love To Come Alive...
And We'll Send the Lucky Winner There!

Silhouette wants to take you wherever
your happy ending can come true.

Here's how to enter: Tell us, in 100 words or less,
where you want to go to make your love come alive!

In addition to the grand prize, there will be 200
runner-up prizes, collector's-edition book sets
autographed by one of the Silhouette anniversary
authors: **Nora Roberts, Diana Palmer,
Linda Howard** or **Annette Broadrick**.

DON'T MISS YOUR CHANCE TO WIN!
ENTER NOW! No Purchase Necessary

Silhouette®
Where love comes alive™

Name: _____

Address: _____

City: _____ State/Province: _____

Zip/Postal Code: _____

Mail to Harlequin Books: **In the U.S.**: P.O. Box 9069, Buffalo, NY
14269-9069; **In Canada**: P.O. Box 637, Fort Erie, Ontario, L4A 5X3

*No purchase necessary—for contest details send a self-addressed stamped envelope to:
Silhouette's 20th Anniversary Contest, P.O. Box 9069, Buffalo, NY, 14269-9069 (include
contest name on self-addressed envelope). Residents of Washington and Vermont may
omit postage. Open to Cdn. (excluding Quebec) and U.S. residents who are 18 or over.
Void where prohibited. Contest ends August 31, 2000.

PS20CON_R